HARD BOUGHT LOVE

HARD BOUGHT LOVE

P.I.V.O.T. LAB CHRONICLES™ BOOK SIX

MICHAEL ANDERLE

LMBPN Publishing
PMB 196, 2540 South Maryland Pkwy
Las Vegas, NV 89109

First US Edition, December, 2020
(Previously published as a part of *Choosing What Matters*)
eBook ISBN: 978-1-64971-380-3
Print ISBN: 978-1-64971-381-0

CHAPTER ONE

The first time Dotty had been in Insea, her avatar had been a young dwarven woman, a caravan guard who knew little about the world around her. She had soaked up the legends of the city—and had done her damnedest to eat her way through every food stand she could find.

She hadn't come close.

This time, she was determined to rectify that. When she swept out of the alley she'd materialized in, she hurried directly to the nearest food stall, which wafted smells of something spiced and fried.

As she walked, she noticed people turn to look at her, and only then did she notice her outfit. It could be defined as "a red dress," but the phrase didn't do the garment justice. It could be more accurately termed a construction rather than a garment, although she thought *contraption* might also work. She raised one glittering hand and layers of sheer silk fell away from her arm while others—tethered to her jeweled bracelets and rings— billowed prettily.

She spent so much time admiring the elegant fall of her

sleeves that it took a gust of wind for her to notice the front of her dress.

There wasn't much of one, unfortunately.

"Prima," she said before she could stop herself. Several people looked at her with interest and she whisked herself into an alley.

"What?" the AI asked. *"I think you look nice. I looked up all kinds of costumes from fantasy games so I could make you a good one. I even toned it down for you."*

"This…is what you would call toned down?" She stared at the diamonds, the silk, the gold thread, and the exposed skin. If it weren't so perfectly warm in Insea, she would have noticed all of this much sooner.

"I could show you some reference art. Would you prefer something more practical?"

Dotty was about to snap that yes, of course, she wanted something more practical. However, several ideas came to her in close succession.

"Is it possible for the dress to fall or…come off or anything?"

"You can take it off if that's what you mean."

"I *mean*, will it flutter in the breeze and show everyone in Insea…well, everything?"

"Oh. No. All the pieces that need to stay on will do so. You see how the sleeves are off your shoulders but they don't slide down? I was very proud of that."

"I was worried about the pieces closer to the center," she muttered, "but yes, I do see that. Er, could I have a mirror?"

"Done," Prima said promptly. A mirror appeared, suspended in midair in the narrow area.

She turned and examined her dress as she did so. Red silk clung to her torso and draped from her hips in perfect folds that billowed and swirled as she moved. Her arms, if held at her sides, were shielded by capelike sleeves of sheer silk attached to her upper arms with tiny diamonds. This being a video game, there did not need to be any unpleasant adhesive or biting hems.

The AI had remembered all her favorites for combat as well. Two sheaths of metal across her forearms looked purely ornamental like faux armor, but when she looked closer, she saw that the decorative flourishes hid two long, wickedly sharp daggers with ornate hilts at her elbows. She drew them both at once and they came out whisper-quiet.

Good. She had discovered a talent for magic, not to mention a love of it, but it was always wise for a lady to be armed. As far as she was concerned, her grandmother—who had been fond of saying that all a lady needed for armor was good manners—could kick rocks.

Gems glittered at her fingers, neck, and ears, and her golden-brown hair was held back in a crown of braids. The hairstyle was the same as she had worn on her wedding day, but she hadn't had rubies and golden pearls woven into it on that occasion.

The woman in the mirror blushed.

"You should say it," Prima said.

"Say what?"

"That you look good."

Unexpectedly, tears trembled on her lashes. Harry had told her that she looked beautiful every morning and had said the same things as Prima. He wanted her to say it, too. Dotty, as she had done every morning while Harry was alive, shook her head wordlessly but she was smiling.

"You are smiling and also sad?"

"Yes, Prima." Dotty made another turn in front of the mirror —it *was* fun to have a dress that swished, no matter how scandalous it might be—and stepped out of the alley.

The smell of food was driving her *crazy.*

What she finally walked away with was a paper cone filled with a jumble of things that seemed to include fried potatoes, corn, onions, and peppers, although that seemed to be only the start of the ingredients. She held it carefully away from her dress.

"Yes," the AI said before she could ask, *"you can spill on it and I'll make sure it doesn't get dirty."*

"You're wonderful," she replied with her mouth already full. "Oh. Hot. Oof."

"Too spicy?"

"No, not after the orc village." In her second incarnation within the world of PIVOT, she had spent time as an orc. The range of orcish foods included far too much dried fish, as well as a stew that was spicy enough to make her pray for death. She took another bite of the potato mixture. "This is merely hot—temperature-wise. Oooh. I like this."

She ate as she strolled. The potato was soft on the inside, gloriously fried on the outside, and deliciously mingled with other pieces of vegetable. She only wished she had pan bread to eat with it. Before long, it was finished and she looked around for a trash bin.

Did fantasy cities *have* trash bins?

Slowly, she pivoted and looked at the street corners. She located nothing close by, but she had passed a little park a few streets back. Perhaps she should go there and check. She stood out of the way of a carriage, rolled her eyes at the rude yells from the driver and the extravagantly-dressed noble inside, and set off.

While she was at it, she should look for another snack. Dotty licked her fingers as she walked. The shoes Prima had given her were made of the same red silk and managed to not pinch her feet at all. In the real world, her feet *always* pinched in shoes, but she was more than happy to not have the game be accurate in this regard. There were certain aspects of her youth she wasn't keen to relive.

One street over from the park, she saw an alley that cut through into a shaded arbor. She ducked into the narrow space, thanking whoever had come up with the idea of a city made of one block of stone. It meant alleys without puddles or crumbling paving stones.

Two men stepped out of an alcove and she stopped in her tracks, her skirts swirling around her. This wasn't the Insea she'd experienced before. Now that she thought about it, though, she remembered the way the other citizens had looked at her—unfriendly and even annoyed. There were so many bodyguards now and people on street corners in ragged clothes. She had seen bands of armed soldiers with no livery—mercenaries for hire, she realized, and none of them seemed to be short of coin.

What had happened there?

"Look, Eto," one of them said to the other. "It's a noblewoman out for a midday stroll." His head was shaved and his beard was very neat—which made the scar that ran through it all the more noteworthy. Dotty could see the muscles beneath his clothes.

"What a kind thing," the other one said. He was taller, with eyes that were so heavy-lidded, they seemed to disappear. Like the other man, he kept his beard neat. He strolled toward her. "It's nice for the nobles to show us how they live, don't you think, Jel?"

"That I do, Eto. That I do." The man with the black beard circled her. He extended his hand to touch the diamonds. "What a beautiful dress—on a beautiful lady, of course."

"Thank you," she said icily.

Both men laughed.

"There now, little lady," Jel said. "There's no need to take that tone. We're merely admirers." He drew a dagger slowly out of one sleeve and took care to let it ring against the sheath. "So, why don't we keep this pleasant, hmm? Hand your purse over."

She took one slow step back. Jel followed equally as slowly.

"You really shouldn't do this," she told him. "I don't think it will stay pleasant."

"Is she threatening us?" he asked Eto.

"You know, I think she is," his comrade replied and strolled past him toward the mouth of the alleyway. "And here we were being so nice to her. Right, Jel? Jel?"

He turned and his jaw dropped. His partner knelt on the ground, wheezing. Both hands clutched his groin—a gesture that had come rather too late—and he tried to catch his breath but failed miserably. Dotty folded her arms and stared at Eto. Her blood was thrumming now.

"I told you," she said quietly, "that you shouldn't do this. I told you it wouldn't stay pleasant."

"Why, you little—" He charged.

She waited until the last possible moment before she leapt sideways over Jel's bent form. The daggers whipped out of their sheathes without a single sound and when she turned, the man had already surged into an attack.

He saw the weapons barely in time to throw himself sideways and she stalked after him. As he scrabbled for his blade, she tripped him. When he sprawled and his fingers located the hilt of the dagger and closed around it, a chunk of mud materialized from nowhere and covered both hand and knife. Eto screamed and the mud vanished, taking the knife with it.

Jel, who seemed to be under the very mistaken impression that he had the element of surprise, uttered a battle cry and lunged at her, knife-first.

He took a dagger to the forearm for his troubles and lost his balance to land hardf. The battle froze into a moment of shocked stillness.

Dotty stomped on his fingers to make him release his weapon and kicked it away. She wrenched hers out of his arm, eliciting a high-pitched scream, and bent slightly to look him in the eyes.

"What's your name? Jel *what?*"

"Jel Estrim." He scrabbled away on his elbows and his knees, trying to clap one hand over the wound in his arm.

"And *you,*" she said, rounding on Eto.

He had tried to sneak up on her, his hands extended to grasp her arms, but he held them up in surrender and leapt back with a shriek.

She stared at him for a moment and tried desperately not to laugh. "And you?" she asked when she was relatively certain she could keep her face straight. "What's *your* surname, *Eto*?"

"Kleim," he said before he winced. He had no doubt been determined to lie and had then forgotten to do so.

As she looked at the other knives, each of them disappeared into a ball of mud and crumbled to dust.

"Well, Mr. Estrim, Mr. Kleim. I suggest you leave before you make anyone else's day unpleasant. In fact, I suggest you *never* make anyone's day unpleasant like this again. If you do—"

"You'll hunt us," Eto snapped. He hauled Jel up and elicited a pained gurgle from his friend. "Yeah, we know."

"Oh, I won't only do that," she said. "I'll not only beat the *crap* out of you myself, I'll track your grandmothers and tell them what you did."

Both of them went white, and she sheathed her weapons again and brushed her dress off before she picked up the wad of paper.

"What are you doing?" Eto asked.

"I'm picking up after myself instead of littering," she said, "because I am a *lady*." She swept toward her destination without looking back.

CHAPTER TWO

The park was, like everything in Insea, carved from the same single block of stone. Some of it was gray, some white, and some pinkish. In the park, it was a golden-white, fashioned into flower beds for real flowers and trees, with little streams running away from a fountain and four statues at the cardinal points on the circular path. Each statue depicted a figure —one orc, one elf, one dwarf, and one human. There were no inscriptions, however, to say if these merely depicted the races or were particular figures from history.

Dotty paused for a moment to look at the orc, a woman holding her arm up either to catch or release a falcon, her hair ornately braided and a leather strap with a claw around her neck. Her dress was nothing like she had seen in the orcish villages she had visited, but a great deal had changed amongst the orcs in the past few centuries.

She found a trash bin—which disappeared conveniently as soon as she had thrown the paper away—and sat on a bench to think things over. It occurred to her that she wasn't entirely sure if she was annoyed that she had been mugged or amused at how the attempt had ended.

Lost in thought, she proceeded to fall off the end of the bench with a yelp of surprise when Justin said, *"Dotty?"*

He rushed to help her up. "Sorry! Sorry." His wide-eyed gaze took in the dress, the hair, and the much younger avatar. "Uh… you look, that is to say…um, no disrespect meant—Tina?"

His girlfriend, who was eating a pizza-esque item, stopped chewing long enough to say, "Nah, it's gonna be much more fun to watch you try to work your way out of this on your own." She swallowed her mouthful. "Hi, Dotty."

"Hello, Tina." She looked at Justin again. "You were saying?"

He was, luckily for him, saved by the arrival of Lyle Stout, a dwarf she had traveled with during her first incarnation in the PIVOT world. It was strange to look down at him instead of being the same height, but she was more concerned with how much she had missed him. Without thought, she threw her arms around him and gave him a hug.

After a moment, she pulled away and realized he was staring at her like she might be a lunatic.

"Do I…know you?" he asked cautiously.

"This is Dotty," Justin explained.

"How many friends do you *have* named Dotty?"

"Same Dotty," Tina confirmed.

"Dotty is…a dwarf." Lyle glanced at her feet as if searching for platform shoes. "She had a real figure the last time I saw her— nice, strong arms to heft a pick-ax and none of this wimpy elf or human business."

"You'd like orcs," Dotty said.

"I've always thought I'd like orcs," he agreed and looked suspiciously at her. "Seriously, though, who are you?"

"Seriously, I'm Dotty. We first met in Berghold, you trained me on the way to Insea, and I fell into a coma after our fight with the elven riders. We interrogated a diplomat together—"

"Shhhh," the dwarf said and waved his hands. "Nothing about that."

She stared at him.

"For legal reasons," Justin said gravely. "Councilor Marwitz was killed during the battle between the elves and the dwarven caravan. Multiple witnesses saw him stabbed by the elven commander."

"Ah," she said. "You learn something new every day, I guess."

"It *is* you, isn't it?" Lyle said finally. "You look…different."

"Don't you agree, Justin?" Tina asked innocently from a bench.

He darted her a look and she grinned at him.

"I'm sorry we're late," a new voice said. Dotty turned to see a young woman with dark hair and leather armor with a man in robes trailing in her wake. "Kural wanted to stop and examine a security spell at one of the weapons shops."

"It was fascinating," Kural said excitedly. "It kept the weapons from being used to harm any of the store's employees—*or* bystanders—but not from being used to harm robbers. You know, I've always said that many of the significant developments in magic come from the commercial sector, not only academia."

"That's nice," Zaara said firmly. She nodded to Dotty. "I'm sorry, you've never met us. I'm Zaara, and this very vague man is Kural, my mentor and a wizard of some renown."

Kural, who had stooped to examine a glyph carved on the bench, straightened for a moment with a wounded expression. "*Some* renown?"

"You'd probably have more if you hadn't spent five years wandering in various disguises," Zaara said, unimpressed by the wounded puppy expression. She looked at Dotty. "Sorry about that. What did you say your name was?"

"We've met, actually," Dotty said. "We fought a fire dragon together. I looked a little different at the time."

The woman's jaw dropped. She looked at her, then at Justin and Lyle, who both nodded. "Oh. Ah. Wow. Okay. Well, it's good to meet you. Again. So, why are we all here?"

"Dotty called us all here," Justin said.

"I did?"

"Yes, you did," Prima said helpfully.

"Yes, I did," she said. She cleared her throat. "Has anyone noticed anything…uh, strange…about Insea?"

"Well, *I* noticed a woman in a red dress kicking the crap out of some muggers," Tina said. She gave her a wink.

"Yes, precisely," she said. "There weren't muggers the last time I was here."

"I don't remember any either," Justin said with a frown. "Callie and Dex were fairly nasty, but it's not like they jumped people in alleys."

"Only in arenas," Tina said, and Dotty was surprised to see her looking deeply angry. There was clearly a story there, but she knew she didn't have time to ask about it.

She filed it away for later and looked at the others. Kural was frowning, although whether it was about this topic or something entirely different, she could not have said. Lyle looked troubled but offered no input besides nodding when Justin spoke.

"There shouldn't be any crime," Zaara said slowly. "Insea is *famously* safe. It's one of the reasons my father wanted me to marry a noble here. He said I could go wandering as much as I wanted and not have to worry about being hurt."

"Well, it would seem he was wrong." Dotty settled on a bench and looked at all of them.

"He *wasn't*," the woman said.

"I just got mugged," Dotty told her. "Tina can corroborate—"

"Ugh," Tina groaned. "Lawyer talk."

"What I *meant*," Zaara said impatiently, "is that when my father said that, it was true."

"So, what happened?" No one seemed to have an immediate answer. "A mass exodus of the city guard?"

Everyone looked at one another before Lyle said, "There's never been a city guard."

"What?" She studied their matching expressions in disbelief. They all seemed fairly sure of the idea, but as far as she could tell, the very concept was cuckoo. A city with no police force?

"Insea has never had an army," Zaara explained. "*Or a city guard.* There are guards in the palace—"

This was familiar ground, and she jumped on it. "For the king? Queen? Person?"

"King," the woman said. She pressed her lips together. "But I don't know, to be honest. No one has ever seen the king."

"No one has…*ever*…seen the king?" Dotty asked. She must be mistaken about what she had heard.

She wasn't, though, because everyone nodded.

"Well, this puts the other elven faction into perspective," Dotty told Lyle. Their first adventure together had involved the yearly shipment of magical goods from Berghold to Insea, an ongoing gesture of thanks from the dwarves to the elves. As far as anyone knew, the elves had enlisted the dwarves' help to build Insea and had then taught the same magic to the dwarves, who used it to build Berghold.

But if the ruler of Insea had never been seen, it made a great deal of sense why a new faction of elves would jockey for power. In fact, she thought, it was more interesting that it hadn't happened sooner—a fact she shared, only to get blank looks from Lyle, Zaara, and Kural.

"It's always been like that," Zaara said.

"No visible monarch, no guards, no army, and no wars," Dotty said. She looked at Justin and Tina, who both frowned in consternation. That was a relief, as she had begun to feel like she was going crazy. "And you never thought that was weird?"

"Well, think about it," Lyle said. "It's not easy to get an army to Insea with those narrow roads."

"Yeah, you told me that last time. It doesn't make sense, though. Insea isn't equipped for defense, there's no strong government in place, and no one is visibly running it at all. Why hasn't anyone tried to take it over? Hell, why haven't the *nobles* staged a coup?"

"I…" The three natives of the game shrugged their shoulders.

"One moment." She turned and raised an eyebrow at the sky. "Prima, the answer doesn't happen to be that all of them are morons, does it?"

"*No.*" The AI laughed.

"I merely wanted to make sure," she said. She pivoted to the others again. "Okay. You all seem like a group of fairly smart people."

"*And Justin,*" Prima interjected.

"Hey!" he protested.

Dotty struggled to not laugh. "Do other nations have wars?" she asked.

"Well, yes," Lyle said.

"Merely not Insea," she said and waited for the nods. "So doesn't it strike you as odd that there's never been any strife related to Insea? And more to the point, that *none of you think it's weird?*"

An awestruck silence followed her challenge. Dotty exchanged a look with Tina, who contemplatively consumed what seemed to be a magically regenerating slice of pizza. She would have to ask her where to get some of that.

"But now," Kural said slowly, "something is happening."

"Yes," she confirmed.

"Which is why the Master of Ceremonies is trying to train the populace of Insea to serve as warriors," Justin said suddenly. "He said he needed me. After the championship, he said I must find more warriors from my land."

"So the Master of Ceremonies knew something was coming," Dotty said thoughtfully, "and now, things are starting to go wrong in large and small ways all across the world. And there's one thing none of the rest of you know, I think."

In quick strokes, she outlined the story she had heard from

the dragons she fought near the orcish village. At some point, centuries before, several dragons had decided to pose as gods. They divided the tribes and made the orcs offer regular sacrifices to them. Their claim was that this was justified and, when she explained to them that it was horseshit, they had told her another dragon had given its life for peace and prosperity in Insea.

When she finished, Kural leapt to his feet and began to pace. She opened her mouth with questions and Zaara waved frantically at her to be quiet. The other woman moved to whisper in her ear.

"He can be absolutely infuriating and he tends to focus on the wrong thing in a fight, but the man has been alive for over three hundred years, and he knows a *lot*. From experience, I'd say to let him think."

Dotty sat, waited, and twiddled her fingers. It felt a little weird to do that in this extraordinary dress. She felt as if she should hold a tiny crystal glass of a rare liqueur and glide around a ballroom but instead, there she was in a very staid, normal park with a strange group eating pizza and chatting about the downfall of the world.

"Here is my guess," Kural said at last. He linked his hands behind his back and began to pace in a much more measured way. "First, I should say that I can confirm the stories of Insea being founded by a dragon—let us not go into *how* I know, but I do know. However, I am beginning to think I missed some rather important details." He continued to walk, his hands behind his back. "There were many old stories of elven shamans who communed with dragons. Some of the stories are rather inappropriate, but *some*—"

"Wait…wait." Tina held a hand out. "Inappropriate *how*?"

Everyone looked at her.

"We all wondered," she said with great dignity. "But, fine. Be boring." She gestured at the wizard to continue.

"Some," he resumed with a sideways look at her, "were about

dragons and elves going further in magic than either race had gone separately. I wonder if one such partnership fueled the creation of Insea. It would explain why the city has always been believed to be an elven creation and why the elves were able to teach some of the same magic to the dwarves. But it would also explain why this magic has not been replicated since. It needs not only a great deal of power but a truly extraordinary magician with an amazing amount of power."

Dotty looked around. "So…did the elf *kill* the dragon?"

"Oh, no," Kural assured her. "A dragon who could provide this much power would…hmm, how to explain it? I doubt there would be anything on earth that could compel it to do anything. No, what it did here, it did willingly—and I would guess that it not only helped create the spell but until recently, *maintained* it."

Everyone frowned.

"What happened recently?" Justin asked finally.

"I have no idea," the wizard said promptly. "There are a great many questions we have to answer, and if we are on the right track, I would say we have very little time in which to answer them. To the palace, everyone. At once."

"As long as we can stop for pizza," Dotty said.

"Agreed," Lyle chimed in.

Kural shook his head. "Fine. But you eat while we walk, and we also need to plan. We'll need to infiltrate the castle."

"I'll help," the dwarf said.

Everyone winced.

"You're not…" Justin said and seemed to try to be diplomatic. "Um…"

"We all have our strengths," Zaara said with a pained smile.

"And yours is *not* subtlety," Dotty said before the rest of the youngsters could tie themselves in any more knots.

"I know that," Lyle said. "That's why I'm offering to be the diversion."

They relaxed as one.
"Better," Justin said.

CHAPTER THREE

Nick took a big bite of his bagel as he wove between the pods in the lab. For the past few months, only one pod had been used at a time, excluding temporary visitors to the world of PIVOT. Right now, there were three patients with three more coming over the next few weeks, and the lab was already an almost unbearable crush.

Also, with all the monitoring equipment beeping, it sounded like a robot convention.

He flipped the second-to-last page of his printout and kept reading as he walked. He was finishing the bagel when he arrived at the row of desks that overlooked the labs. Amber and Jacob were already there, talking quietly over a cup of coffee, and DuBois was asleep at his desk.

The group had joked that they weren't sure if the doctor had a place to stay in New York, but they began to think the joke might be reality. They had started dropping increasingly desperate hints that they had pull-out couches and air mattresses available, but so far, he seemed perfectly content to sleep at his desk.

Maybe *he* was a robot, Nick thought. He rolled his desk chair to where his partners were. "Sorry I'm late. I thought I started at the normal time—"

"You aren't," Amber said. "We both got here early."

"Oh. That explains it." He shook the printout and poppy seeds from the bagel drifted to the floor. "So. Mattis file?"

"Right." Amber leaned forward to snatch her copy off the desk. "You said you had concerns?"

"We have three patients now," he pointed out, "and it is *overwhelming*. We had to institute a checklist for casual conversations to make sure we weren't talking about different people. It was a nightmare. I almost gave Jenna heart failure the other day when I was talking about Dotty and she was talking about Kyle. We have three more coming soon and this lab will be a circus. I honestly don't think we need another person right now."

She nodded and looked at Jacob for his input.

He rubbed his forehead wearily. "I can't argue with that. The thought of another person is…intimidating. I've literally had nightmares about adding the next three."

"Nightmares?" Amber said.

"Yeah. Kind of? I don't know. I dreamed I was stuck in this loop of doing the hourly readout checks and no one else was here. I kept going to start one and then remembered I hadn't finished the last and I never seemed to be done. Anyway, I woke up and threw up." He took a sip of coffee and stared into the distance. "I'm fairly sure my neighbor thinks I'm a junkie."

Nick snickered. "Yeah. So, that's my point. We don't need Jacob waking up in the middle of the night to hurl. He's already lost too much weight since we moved here."

"Yeah, I don't know what happened with that." He scratched at his chin, where there was a few days' worth of stubble.

"You're way too stressed," Amber said. She looked at Nick and gestured to herself. "We all are. Although if I could upgrade to the version of stress where you lose weight instead of gain it, I'd like to do that now, please."

"Seconded," Nick said glumly.

Jacob laughed and rubbed his head. "If you'd told me six months ago that I'd lose my mind because we had too *many* patients, I'd have said you were crazy."

"Agreed." She shook her head. "But we *are* taking on too much. I think we need to accept that we can't be involved in every case the same way. What that looks like, I don't know."

"We're engineers," he said morosely. "We should be where the data is."

Nick patted his hand. "We'll find a solution. So, are we agreed, though? We don't need another patient right now?"

"Well, I don't know." Jacob looked at his copy of the printout.

"Don't go all bleeding heart on me," his friend warned him.

"You're one to talk. Also, we…kind of run a company that rehabilitates people. The bleeding heart is a feature, not a bug."

"Okay," Nick grinned. "But if you keep losing weight like this, you only have a few weeks left before a stiff breeze can blow you away."

"Fair. We'll think of something." Jacob waved his hands. "In the meantime—mmf."

Amber had inserted a piece of a donut into his open mouth. Jacob stared at her and she shrugged. He grimaced, chewed, swallowed, and took the rest of it off her plate.

"As I was *saying,* I would say this case is about twenty-five percent bleeding heart and seventy-five percent rabid curiosity."

"So we're doing this?" Nick asked Amber. "We're doing the stupid thing and taking on more work?"

"Well, I…" She looked at him over the rim of her coffee cup. "Have we *ever* done the smart thing?"

"Fair." He pivoted to where the other man pinned pieces of paper onto a corkboard. "I guess we're doing this. At least it's an interesting case."

They were all interesting cases. That was what made it so difficult to say no to new applicants even when there was no hope in hell that the pods would help them. Not only were the variety of conditions interesting, the families had inevitably gone through an endless parade of specialists who hadn't been able to help and they were desperate.

Even when Nick knew he couldn't help, he *hated* sending the form letters to tell people so. He secretly thought it was the piece of the job that weighed most heavily on his friend. It was the ICU costs for his grandmother that had inspired them to use the pods for this in the first place, and he seemed to care about each potential case as if they were his own family.

Jacob had pinned a picture on the board—a girl with wavy dark hair and a small mouth, clearly uncomfortable in front of the camera as well as in her collared shirt and blazer, which looked like part of a school uniform.

Next to her, he pinned a picture of a boy with the same dark hair and eyes but otherwise, a very different face. Hers was a pale oval while his seemed to be all angles and planes.

"Taigan and Jamie Mattis," he announced.

"I thought they were twins."

"Not all twins are identical," Amber pointed out. "And…well, a boy and a girl won't be."

"I suppose so." Nick frowned.

"Taigan has a condition that literally has no name," Jacob said. "Since she was four years old, she's fallen into coma-like states. They vary in length between a couple of days and a few weeks, usually, although right now, she's in one that has gone on for five months."

Amber shook her head. "Those poor parents."

"Those poor siblings," Nick said.

"Her siblings?" She looked at him. "I guess. When I was little, I think I'd have given almost anything to have my brothers shut up for a couple of weeks." She paused. "Too dark? Are we allowed to joke about this?"

"I'll give it a pass," Jacob said wryly, "but I have a famously bad sense of humor so don't take my word for it."

"I merely mean," Nick said and drew their attention to him again, "that it's hard to be the sibling everyone forgets about. And she has a twin, so it's probably worse for him than it would be for a normal sibling. But don't they also have an older sister?"

"Yes." Amber flipped through the information and searched for the name. "Emilia. She's nineteen."

"Yeah," he said. "She's supposed to be in college, spreading her wings, and I bet when she calls home, all she hears about is her sister. I wouldn't be surprised if she's as resentful as hell."

"I hadn't thought of that." She chewed her lip.

"Yeah," Jacob said, "but that's also not something we can fix."

"I'm merely pointing it out." Nick scanned the notes. "I have to say, they don't seem very hopeful."

"At this point, why would they be?" the other man countered. "But I'll go out on a limb and guess that the twin heard about this and suggested it to them. He's a seventeen-year-old boy and probably the most likely one in the family to do more research on PIVOT. And if he wants to get involved—"

"What about the older sister?" Nick asked.

"Yeah, it could have been her, too." He shrugged. "Or maybe the mom or dad saw one of the interviews. We had a shit-ton of publicity. I merely…" He looked at the board. "The twin thing."

His partners exchanged a look.

"I think the twins might be a key to each other," Jacob said. "On the face of it, this isn't something we can expect to fix, right? It's a chronic condition. But this has been five months and she isn't coming out. Even if it's getting worse, even if we *can't* fix it, we can give them a way to communicate with her and her a way to not be locked in. And if—" He shut his mouth with a snap.

"Okay." Nick leaned forward, his elbows on his knees. "I want to be clear on something before we go any further."

"Yeah?" Jacob knew him well enough to be wary.

"We modified PIVOT to help with immediate, chronic, trauma-related incidents," he said. "People like Justin, who had trauma-induced comas. People with strokes."

The other man remained silent. His arms were folded and he looked tense.

"We *aren't* doctors," Nick said. "We are merely people introducing a new technology for doctors to *use,* and no doctors have said they can help Taigan."

"Yeah," Jacob said. "But it's not like this is pumping her full of some experimental drug. We do a trial run and see if she integrates with the world."

"Yeah, I know." Nick leaned back in his chair and regarded him firmly. "But *you* want to fix her."

"I can't fix her," the other man said instantly.

"Yeah, that's the smart answer. That's the *right* answer. But what I said was that you *want* to fix her, and I think I'm right about that." He raised his eyebrows and pressed his palms together. "What you said about the twin thing—you think you can develop a plotline with Jamie to pull Taigan out of this coma and then somehow, she'll never fall into one again."

Amber looked from one to the other. She didn't say anything.

Jacob's shoulders hunched. He didn't look at either of them and simply waited for this to blow over.

Unfortunately for him, they had both been his friend for years and they knew this tactic. They were also both willing to wait for him to speak. Amber crossed her legs in her desk chair with one knee against an armrest and Nick leaned back and sipped his coffee.

"*Fine,*" Jacob said when it became clear they wouldn't cooperate. "Yes. Okay. I hope that if she and her brother can work her out of this coma and maybe a couple more, she'll…start to train her brain to do it without the pod. That's my hope." He glared at Nick. "And I don't see why it even matters."

"It matters because you *cannot* promise that to her parents,"

Amber said. "You can't even hint at it. It would be incredibly cruel to give them hope when we have no idea if we can follow through. We don't even know if she can integrate with the game yet. This isn't a trauma-induced coma. We might not be able to reach her at all."

"And it matters," Nick said gently, "because we might do good work and get her out of this coma and you'll still feel like you failed. I don't want you to hold out hope that you can save this family all on your own."

Their friend looked for a moment like he might blow up at them, but his shoulders sagged and he nodded. "I know I have no right to hope for it," he said. "I only…"

"You're hoping it anyway," Nick said. "I know, buddy. I've known you for years. Look, let's invite them in. But keep in mind what your expectations are. You're already stressed, okay? You don't need to add 'solving medical mysteries' to your checklist right now."

He nodded, but when he went back to his computer, Nick sighed.

Amber was right. None of them ever made the smart choice and their entire company was based on trying to do the impossible. None of them could resist an unsolved problem. He knew that before long, despite their best efforts, all of them would try to solve Taigan's condition and they'd blame themselves if they couldn't.

CHAPTER FOUR

Kural marched them to the royal palace at a rapid pace. He muttered constantly and looked entirely deranged, and Zaara had to explain that he was trying to contact a friend inside the palace.

"So," Justin said around a mouthful of the pizza-like snack, "like magical Bluetooth."

"Blue..tooth?" The woman ran her tongue over her teeth, clearly unnerved by the idea of blue ones.

Dotty waved her hand to tell her not to bother. She'd have explained it but to do so, she would have to stop eating the pizza and she absolutely wouldn't do that. The crust was impossibly thin but somehow still supported the sauce, which was creamy and spicy in equal measure. What was *in* it, she didn't know—it might have been meat or vegetables—but it was so delicious that she didn't care about being unable to identify it.

And the *cheese*. She took another bite and her eyes drifted closed happily as she savored the perfect amount of melty, gooey cheese. How was it possible to desperately crave something while you were eating it?

In the next moment, she walked directly into a lamppost and shook her head. Another mouthful of pizza helped.

A moment later, Kural said loudly, "*Excellent.*"

Everyone jumped and looked at him with identical chipmunk expressions, their cheeks stuffed with pizza.

"*You all look great, by the way.*"

Dotty didn't bother to respond to Prima. She raised her eyebrows at the wizard in query.

"Jaco will have an escort waiting for us at the palace," he said.

"Wait." Lyle swallowed a bite of pizza. "So what do I do?"

Kural frowned at him. "You come with us."

"I don't get to make a diversion?"

"You don't *have* to make a diversion," Justin corrected him. "Making diversions isn't something you want to do, is it?"

"Yeah. It is."

"Oh." The young man seemed to try to think of something to say. Eventually, he gave up and began to eat again. "Does anyone else want to try?"

"I got this," Dotty said. "Lyle, if you behave yourself, I'll buy us all a feast tonight and you can have a barrel of beer to yourself."

"Two barrels," the dwarf said promptly.

"Done." She looked at Justin. "See?"

"You're not very strict for a grandmother," he said.

"Different situations call for different solutions." She took another bite of pizza and hummed in pleasure. "Plus, I don't have to deal with the fallout of this one."

They were met at the gates by a young man in black robes. His sash was embroidered in gold and the entire ensemble fit him badly. He looked, to her jaded eye, like a young man who was still having growth spurts and wasn't quite sure where his elbows and knees were anymore.

She had certainly missed having a healthy body, but she did not miss adolescence in the slightest. All she could remember of that time was the almost painful awkwardness.

The young man examined their ragtag group and didn't seem quite sure what to say. He took in Lyle's battle-worn clothing, Zaara's long daggers, and Tina's unimpressed smirk. It became clear the longer he looked that he tried very hard to *not* look at her red dress and its contents.

In her youth, she would have been nervous under anyone's stare when wearing it. In her middle age, she would have been wryly amused by the attention—and more pleased than she wanted to admit. Now, in her old age, all she could think was that they were wasting time.

"Young man," she said before she remembered that she looked about twenty herself, "will you take us to Jaco?"

"Uh. Yes." He attempted awkwardly to keep his gaze averted when he spoke and now, a blush rose blotchily across his neck and face.

Kural either took pity on the poor boy or he was entirely oblivious. Dotty couldn't tell which. He smiled and swept forward, urging their guide to turn and lead them into the palace. "Now, what has Jaco been up to lately?" he asked as they walked.

She smiled and took the opportunity to look around with real interest. The golden-white stone continued, shot through with ripples of gray. It had been carved into an impossibly thin, ornate screen above the entry. Under Insea's warm sun, the awning cast dappled shadows on the broad staircase that led to the castle.

There were still no guards. Dotty had expected to see them lining the staircase or at least patrolling it, but no one was there except their little group.

In a way, it was sad. This was a massive place—it seemed like something that should be full and bustling—but it was clear even from the entrance that it was an old relic. No one came there, not petitioners and not nobles. The fact that there was no dust on the stairs was jarring, though. There really should be. Worse, the sense of emptiness hung in the air.

The rest of the palace only seemed worse. The group moved

through massive, vaulted hallways filled with arches that reminded her of trees. There was no art on the walls, however, or rugs on the floors. It seemed as if no one had ever inhabited it at all.

And there were no servants. Two guards had nodded to their guide at the main door and they had seen one patrol since then, but nothing else.

She shivered.

"What's wrong?" Zaara asked her quietly. She cleared her throat. "Ah, would you like my cloak? That dress doesn't look...warm."

"It's not that," she said and darted another uncomfortable glance at their surroundings. "This whole place seems *wrong.*"

"Wrong how?" the woman whispered.

Dotty only shrugged helplessly. She couldn't put the feeling into words.

They met Jaco in a receiving room with one wall entirely open to the gardens outside. In pleasant contrast to what they'd seen thus far, there was furniture, but it only served to remind them of how bare the rest of the palace looked.

He dismissed his attendant, who withdrew with a curious look over his shoulder. The man watched him leave and ushered their small group to the open wall—and away from prying ears, she guessed.

"A very interesting message," he said to Kural. "Asking about a 'certain dragon' and the founding of Insea? Which 'certain dragon' would this be?"

"The dragon you told me about several months ago," the wizard said in weary good humor. "They all know about it, so you can spare yourself the trouble of trying to mislead them."

Jaco sighed. "You were always terrible at keeping secrets."

"Mmm. But now...I'm beginning to think you didn't tell me the whole story." He studied his old friend steadily. His gaze took in every flicker, but he looked at Dotty to confirm what he had seen.

She nodded.

"So, it's true," Kural said gently.

Their host looked from one to the other. He cleared his throat.

"Jaco," Dotty said. "It is clear that something is wrong in Insea." She stepped closer. "Those of us here want only good for the city and have nothing invested in spreading wild tales or betraying confidences."

"Mmm." He turned to look at Justin, Tina, and Lyle. "Three former contestants in the tournament, a wizard, a wizard's apprentice who wears armor and knives, and…you. Who are you?"

"It depends on who you ask," Dotty said, amused. "To some, I'm a dwarven *zauberer* defending the caravan from Berghold. To others, I am a shaman-in-training of the orcish earth tribe and slayer of two godsprings."

Jaco raised an eyebrow. "And if I ask *you*?"

"I am someone who prefers to not be mugged in alleyways," she said tartly. "Which I was this morning. And I am someone who will go to rather extraordinary lengths to fix injustices."

"I promised I would bring warriors back," Justin said from behind them. "Dotty is one of them."

"Mmm." The Master of Ceremonies looked at each of them before he focused on the garden, his expression thoughtful.

"You've already decided to tell us," Dotty said impatiently. "You need the help and the secret is killing you. You might as well spit it out. None of us are getting any younger, and the problem *clearly* isn't solving itself."

He gave her a surprised look and cleared his throat. "Fine. Er…where to start. That's…rather the problem."

Everyone waited, some more patiently than others.

"Insea was founded by a dragon," Jaco said at last. He linked his hands behind his back and bounced nervously on his feet. "Or a… partnership…between a dragon and an elf." He blushed a bright red.

Tina gestured as if to say, "This is what I was talking about." Justin lowered his head into one hand, and Zaara struggled openly to keep her composure.

"They were both quite accomplished wizards," the man explained, having recovered his composure. "They imagined a world that would never know war or famine, one where all would be fed and able to pursue their heart's desire."

"A utopia," Dotty murmured.

"Precisely," he said. "But the spells went…wrong. To make a very long story short, their utopia never came to pass in the way they had meant it to do."

"They rarely do," she said, almost amused. She saw the stricken look on his face, however, and frowned. "What happened?"

"The elf died," he said simply. "How, I am not certain. Gos'hauke never told me. I think he could not bear to remember."

"Gos'hauke is…the dragon," she said to clarify.

He nodded. His jaw was clenched so tightly that she could see a muscle jumping in his cheek.

"He's dead," she said quietly, "isn't he?"

Jaco nodded. To her surprise, tears glittered in his eyes. "Four months ago," he said. His voice broke on the words. "Give or take." He seemed to attempt to salvage some shred of his demeanor and took a deep breath. "You see, they had planned that they would imbue the city with a…yearning for a leader. A strong, just leader."

"I don't understand," Kural said.

"The city would *call* its leader," he explained, "and release them when their service was no longer needed. It would not be a monarchy made of a bloodline, and the transfer of power would be peaceful."

"They thought—" Justin broke off when everyone looked at him. He cleared his throat. "I don't mean to be disrespectful, I honestly don't, but did they truly think it would never go wrong? Power corrupts, right? They say that for a reason. What if a ruler didn't want to leave?"

"I asked the same thing," Jaco said. "They told me the city would keep that from happening." He paused, clearly at war with himself, and then said in a rush, "It would control minds. It must have been intended to do so. And it *has*."

Dotty raised an eyebrow. Now that he said it that way, the whole experiment seemed a little less pleasant. "That's why there aren't wars involving Insea or nobles trying to take control. The city exerts an influence that stops people from doing that."

"Yes," he said bluntly. "Or…it did while Gos'hauke was still alive. As I understand it, if the spell had worked as intended, it would have existed in perpetuity. Unfortunately, when the elf died, they were not able to complete it. They never reached the part where a leader would be called, and the rest—the peace—was something Gos'hauke slowly gave his life to maintain."

"*Ah*," she said. "So the dragons were right when they said that." She explained what she'd been told and said, "And they're right, we didn't complain. But I think part of that is because we didn't know. Gos'hauke also kept anyone from thinking about it too hard."

He nodded. "Yes," he said quietly.

"And now, it's breaking down," she added. "Quickly."

The Master of Ceremonies nodded. "I should have…well, that's the thing. I don't know what I should have done. I'm not meant to be Insea's ruler."

"They could do far worse," Kural said with a flash of humor. "I know you, remember."

The man didn't look remotely interested or amused. He shook his head flatly and sighed. "And the end came more quickly than he expected. I thought he could come up with a plan but too soon, he was gone and I didn't know what to do. I think he would want me to find someone to finish what he—they—started, but…"

Dotty thought she understood what she saw on his face.

"But you're angry," she said. "You feel manipulated and betrayed. You aren't sure what he did was a good plan. And while you are a wizard, you aren't one who could build anything like this. You face the dilemma of whether to give people assured peace or free will."

"Yes," Jaco confirmed softly.

"Kural," she said.

"Yes?"

"You mentioned that the power it would take to do this would be extraordinary. Is there any way we could possibly recreate it and make it work this time?"

Whether the wizard saw where she was going or not, she wasn't sure, but he did not equivocate. He shook his head. "The researcher in me wants to say yes. But…no. I am almost certain we could not."

"Then our path is clear," Dotty stated. "We don't have an ethical dilemma at all—which I, for one, am glad about."

"Yes," Jaco said a little desperately, "but what *do* we do?"

"We begin working for peace," Dotty told him crisply. "The old-fashioned way, mind you, with common interests and face-to-face negotiations. Roll your sleeves up, everyone. This will be some of the hardest work you've ever done."

CHAPTER FIVE

Jaco led them through empty corridors to his study. Dotty walked beside him.

"So, they intended this place to be inhabited," she said.

"Yes." He was subdued. "I miss him, you know. I...do."

She smiled sadly. "But?"

The man glanced at her. "But, indeed. But he didn't truly like us humans and elves as much as he thought he did. If he had loved what we were, he wouldn't have controlled us all."

Her expression neutral, she nodded.

"I've struggled with it," he admitted. "I haven't been comfortable with the idea since I learned what the spell did, but since he died, the doubts have become stronger. His magic...suppressed them. And that seems wrong to me."

"It *is* wrong," she agreed. "That's why you weren't comfortable with it. You said it earlier. He controlled people's minds. That's what this was."

"Yes," he admitted. "And I'm...glad their spell didn't work. I'm not glad that he lost his lover, though. It broke him and he continued to mourn for centuries, but if they'd succeeded, everyone would have lived in a cloud forever."

"That doesn't sound like a struggle," she told him. "Your mind sounds quite clear to me. Or is the struggle simply that you want to think well of him?"

Jaco walked in silence for a moment. "No," he admitted. He looked at her.

"It's…that I can see an argument for renewing the spell."

"*What?*"

"I was grateful when Kural said it couldn't be done. You must understand, I'm not as good a wizard as he is. I never have been so I knew *I* couldn't do it, but I didn't know if it was possible for someone else and—"

"Wait, wait, wait." Dotty stopped, her hand on his arm. Behind them, the others drifted to a halt, too engaged in their discussion to notice why. "You were thinking of renewing the spell?"

The man heaved a sigh. "Yes. And I think, if you consider why for a moment, you'll understand better. You said yourself in that room that there was no dilemma if there was no option. Why did you call it a dilemma?"

She groaned. "Okay, yes, I get it—if the world is at peace, people don't die in wars, and that's good. But you know it would be a terrible thing to do. Controlling people's thoughts?"

"Yes," he agreed readily. "It disgusts me as an idea, it does. But it's not an abstract right now—or it wasn't for me when I thought it might be possible. If I could guarantee that no one would be robbed or murdered, that there would never be any wars or famines…what do you think people would say if they found out I could and I didn't?"

Dotty opened her mouth to retort but bit the words back and thought about it. During her eighty-four years on Earth, she'd lived through more than one war. She had seen people return in boxes, or come back in body but not in spirit, or not come back at all. After one of John's friends was murdered by her husband, she had sat with her son for hours. There was so much pain in the world.

"People like to say that the pain in life gives meaning to the rest," Jaco said, "but none of them have ever had a choice to live any other way."

She shook her head slowly. "I'm glad we don't have a choice," she admitted. Even contemplating this for a moment made her head and her heart go to war.

"Me as well," he said. "When he said no, it was like a great weight had lifted."

They resumed walking until they entered a beautiful room. Silks had been draped to bring the ceiling lower and give it a homey feel, and plush carpets covered the floors. In actuality, it was an ornate room—the kind of place in which she would normally feel uncomfortable touching anything. In there, however, any touches of color or hominess felt cozy. She kicked her shoes off and sank onto one of the couches with a sigh.

Jaco smiled and rang a little bell as he murmured under his breath. An assortment of food appeared on a nearby table, complete with mugs and a steaming pitcher of tea. As the others helped themselves to the food, he dragged a low table closer. He secured a map on it with little weights on the corners which he retrieved from his desk.

"Cool," Justin said. He held a plate piled high with a variety of ornately shaped pastries and dumplings. When people looked confused, he swallowed a mouthful of food and gestured at the map. "I always wanted to be at one of these war-planning meetings."

"Okay, but remember," Tina told him, "this is an *un*-war planning meeting. Anti-war? War un-planning?" She frowned at the sky. "The opposite of a war plan."

"Yes," Dotty said. "That."

She leaned forward to look as she ate a spiced pastry that tasted of cloves and cinnamon. Insea was immediately visible, as it was marked with an ornate ring of golden ink. It took her some time to find Berghold and even longer after that to guess where the orcish lands were.

Jaco retrieved several markers and placed one on Berghold, one in the center of the orcish lands, one in the human lands, one at the northernmost edge of the map, and one in a place that wasn't marked with anything at all. When he saw her looking at it, he smiled bitterly.

"*That* is the so-called capital city of the new elvish faction."

"Oh, those," she said. "I met some of them and killed some of them." She smiled blandly. "Did you know they killed one of the senior dwarven councilors?"

Lyle smothered a snort and fixed his attention on his cup of tea.

"I had heard as much," the man said with enough casualness in his tone that she couldn't tell if he was uninterested or bluffing. He gestured at the board. "Now, these markers represent the major powers of the world—the orcs, the dwarves, the humans, the elves, and the fae."

"The fae?" she asked in surprise. "I didn't know there was a fifth race."

"There might as well not be," Kural said. His nostrils flared. "Nasty, vicious little creatures."

"Some of the only ones who can beat him at games of skill," Jaco confided to the others in a stage whisper.

"They *cheat*," the wizard said.

"Mmm. And you're one of those who know the most about them."

"What's that supposed to mean? Are you suggesting that I cheat, too? Because I don't, I'll have you know. I *never* cheat."

"That wasn't what I meant," the other man said. He smiled. "I meant you're indisputably the best one to meet with them and extend the diplomatic olive branch."

Kural's jaw dropped. "Oh. Oh, no. *Absolutely* not."

"We need someone we can trust and we can trust you. Not to

mention that you can get through the wards you'll need to break to enter the fae lands in the first place."

"They've never bothered anyone in years," he argued in return.

"And we would like to keep it that way," Jaco said promptly. "Enough, Kural. You're going. You should take your apprentice with you."

He snorted. "Her father wants her to stay safe. This is the opposite of that."

"Or you could let her talk for herself before she slits your throat," Dotty suggested.

"I'd second that caution," Justin said.

"Excellent," the Master of Ceremonies said as if everyone had enthusiastically agreed to the plan. "I have several people I can send to the various human settlements."

"Whoa, wait." Justin spread his hands. "Why not us? Me and Tina?"

"Because you don't know anything about the human governments," Zaara said.

"And ye're not so good with th' diplomacy," Lyle added.

"I can be diplomatic! And Tina…will also be there." He looked at her. "Please don't piss off any diplomats like you did in Berghold."

"Then they'd better not cheat at dice."

"Don't play dice with anyone!"

"I have a suggestion," Zaara said. Everyone looked at her and she smiled. "Kural and I will accompany Justin and Tina to the human lands, give them an overview, and introduce them to relevant leaders. They will stay to establish diplomatic relations while Kural and I continue north to the fae lands." She nodded to Justin and Tina. "Humans recognize power and bloodline and they have very specific ideas of other human nations. Justin and Tina aren't from any of the rival noble families, and they'll be introduced by two wizards. It's fairly perfect…if they can pull it off."

"We can pull it off," Justin said dangerously.

"Done," Jaco said promptly.

"Wait, really?" The young man looked unsettled.

"Yes." The Master of Ceremonies tapped the map. "Speed is of the essence and there are very few people I trust with the knowledge of why this is so essential. Also, the humans are famous for in-fighting. All you need to do is convince them that Insea is more concerned with its problems than with theirs—and that we're training a guard force to combat those internal problems. Therefore, it presents a dangerous populace and an undesirable target."

Dotty leaned back in her seat. She was enjoying this.

"That leaves us with the dwarves, the elves, and the orcs," Jaco said. "Dotty, you told me you'd worked with two orcish villages. I assume you're one of the best to go to them."

"Well…" She shrugged. "They think I'm dead and they certainly won't recognize me. But they are speaking of uniting again, which means we definitely should talk to them about diplomatic relations. And I suppose I also know a good deal about their culture. Okay. I'll go there."

"I'm reluctant to send anyone alone," he said, "and I must remain here. I propose that Dotty and Lyle go both to Berghold and the orcish territories. Dotty has done a valuable service for Berghold and will therefore be welcome, and if orcs are likely to respect any other race, it's the dwarves."

"What about the elves?" she asked.

The man paused and looked uncertain. "That…is a puzzle and one I am not certain of how best to address. I will think on it and send exploratory messages." He stood. "All of you, take the next day to prepare. You leave at dawn the day after tomorrow, and I'll do all I can to speed you on your way."

CHAPTER SIX

Nick's first impression of the Mattis family was of lanky height. Jamie Mattis and his father shared a tall build that wasn't quite filled out. While Simon moved with studied efficiency, his hair entirely gray but his manner spry, Jamie still moved like he wasn't quite sure what to do with his height.

Emilia Mattis, the oldest child, was the shortest of the group but he would guess from a distance that she was still five-six or taller. Even her mother Aimee, whose round face and straight black hair spoke of her Chinese heritage, was unusually tall.

His second impression, as the group scrambled out of the taxi, was that they had recently been in a fight of some kind. Emilia was tight-lipped, her shoulders hunched, and she lagged behind the rest of the group as they approached the PIVOT headquarters, while Jamie hung back and spoke urgently to her.

Whatever she said to him, he looked like a whipped puppy when they reached the lobby.

Nick had to take a moment to steady himself before he stepped forward to greet the parents. He couldn't think about the two miserable children trailing in their wake without remembering too many moments from his childhood.

It hurt to be forgotten.

"Mr. Mattis, Mrs. Mattis." He nodded to them and held a hand out for them to shake. "I'm Nick Ryan, one of the founders of PIVOT. Thank you for coming."

"Thank you for showing us around," Simon said. Nick formed a snap judgment in that moment of someone who liked to do things correctly. He would be polite and engaging. He had come here today because he owed it to his daughter to try to find a cure for her condition.

And it would be killing him that no matter how many specialists he'd seen, nothing had worked so far.

"We appreciate your work," Aimee added. She wore her hair cropped short and spoke in a southern drawl that surprised him. "These are Taigan's siblings, Jamie and Emilia. Jamie, Emilia, this is Mr. Ryan."

He saw the resentment flare in Emilia's eyes at being treated like a child but she, like her brother, shook his hand and muttered a polite greeting.

"Why don't we start with the lab?" he asked. He moved to the elevators and made a mental note to allow each of the Mattises time to ask private questions. The children, at least, looked like they would benefit from the opportunity to be away from their parents. On a whim, he added, "If the two of you would like to stay on to ask more questions after the tour, perhaps we could have one of the laboratory assistants show Jamie and Emilia the city."

Emilia only leaned into the corner of the elevator and sighed, her arms folded, as her mother shook her head.

"Oh, no, they can stay. It's no trouble."

I tried, Nick wanted to tell the girl. He guessed that she and Jamie were kept on a fairly tight leash. Their mother would inevitably be quite cautious about their safety, what with the unpredictable nature of their sister's condition.

With Amber in a meeting with the Diatek accountants and

Jacob meeting with Anna Price, Diatek's CEO, he was in charge of the tour. He had to admit, despite being nervous about having been acquired by a defense contractor, he was very glad to be able to show off this high-end, expensively outfitted laboratory instead of the dingy set of offices PIVOT had once rented.

Simon and Aimee Mattis would *never* have agreed to have Taigan treated in that facility.

Nick showed them the row of pods, sleek and white, beeping with LEDs and printouts, and each attended by several assistants in crisp, white lab coats. In the well-lit lab, the pods looked unthreatening and even comforting.

"As you can see," he said, "we have several people in the pods at present."

"Patients?" Simon asked.

"PIVOT is doing two branches of research," he said carefully. "The first is recovery care, which is what Justin Williams received. The other is baseline testing, which helps us to understand how people of different demographics interact with the world inside the pods."

"And these…" Simon gestured at the pods.

"Unfortunately, I cannot share information about any of the individuals currently in the pods," he said.

"Ah. My apologies."

"None needed."

"If you're still doing testing…" Aimee interrupted. She looked uncertainly at her husband before she refocused on Nick. "Is it safe to have someone's—I believe you called it 'recovery care'—happen this way? If you don't know how certain people respond to the treatment?"

Simon looked uncomfortable but he nodded.

"That's a good question, and I'm afraid I can't offer you any guarantees. What we hope is that the treatment we offer will supplement the existing set of options—that it will merely be another option doctors can turn to if they believe it is appropriate for an individual patient. Should you choose to move forward with this, one step would be to speak to Taigan's care team and get a better understanding of whether they believe this is a good option for her."

Aimee hesitated before she nodded.

"So you can't fix her," Emilia said bluntly. Both of her parents looked sharply at her and she shrugged with studied indifference. "What? They all make sure to not promise anything. If they'll take a chunk of money for it, I think they should be honest."

She looked fierce and before her mother or father could reprimand her, Nick spoke.

"I can't imagine how frustrating this has been for you," he told her frankly. "And exhausting. Each time, you're not sure whether to get your hopes up and no one can ever give you guarantees."

If anything, him agreeing with her had made her more suspicious. She stared at him with an unimpressed expression.

"All I can tell you," he continued, "is that, if we'd had the chance, Jacob's grandmother would have been one of the first we tried to help. It was her experience in the ICU that propelled us to use this technology for medical care. We believe that it will get us closer to being able to fix things like comas but right now, we don't know enough to fix problems like that. No one does."

Emilia glared at him for another moment before she looked at the floor. He thought he saw the sheen of tears in her eyes.

You're trying to protect her, he thought. *You're trying to protect all of them. You watch your parents spend all their energy on this, get their hopes up, and get crushed every time. And in the meantime, the whole family is in limbo.*

He couldn't say any of that, though, because he didn't know them well enough. A little despondent, he cleared his throat.

"We've had people come from all around—some heard about Justin's care on the news and some found it because they were already following virtual reality developments. How did PIVOT first come to your attention?"

"Jamie told us about it." Simon still looked deeply displeased with Emilia's outburst but he tried to salvage the situation. He gestured to his son, who looked nervous and miserable now.

The kid was the peacemaker of the family, Nick guessed. He wanted all of them to get along and stop yelling.

And he wanted his twin back. Jacob was right about that.

"What appealed to you about the idea of the pods?" Nick asked Jamie.

"Well, it's—a chance. You know, to…cure her." He nodded awkwardly.

"Yes, but your sister is right. You have all gone through this many times." He nodded at him. "I imagine when you hear about a new treatment, part of you is simply tired of the whole cycle. What made you speak to your parents about this one?" He looked at the boy's face. "You don't have to answer if you don't want to."

Jamie stared at the floor.

"Jamie?" his mother asked. "It's all right. You should tell him whatever it is."

Nick could gladly have strangled her. Nothing he could say would make this better, though. He merely had to wait, but he noticed that even Emilia looked curious.

Finally, Jamie said, "I saw the interview with Justin's mother, where she said…she could go into the game and talk to him. I thought—maybe I could go in. I could help her."

He looked deeply embarrassed. Nick could hear the shame behind the words. *He's thinking, 'I know how childish this is.'*

But Mary and Tina had gone into the game for Justin, and Dotty's family going in to see her had resulted in a measurable change to her endocrine levels and brain activation. Not only did the PIVOT team now know friends and family made a difference, Jamie was right. Who better to go into the world than a twin?

Nick had to stop himself before he did the exact thing he'd warned Jacob about. He couldn't promise anything right now, no matter how much he wanted to.

"Part of why this treatment interests researchers," he explained, "is exactly the kind of thing you're talking about—the ability to communicate with people who are comatose. If your family and your doctors decide to move forward with this, there may be some communication with her. I don't know what that will look like, if so, but I imagine you'll all at least be able to send letters to her and she can send letters back."

For a moment, the family looked completely united. All of them had a yearning look on their faces. Aimee had tears in her eyes and Simon slid his arm around her shoulders, cleared his throat, and looked away.

"Why don't we see more of the facility," Nick said. "I can show you some demos of the game and, if you want, you'll have the option to see one of us interact with the technology live. Or any of you are also free to go into the game if you want to experience it for yourself. There's no need to answer now. It's merely something to think about."

He set off without waiting for a response because he wanted them to think about it rather than feel like they had to commit to anything. Jamie's desperation to get into the game was almost palpable, but the parents would have to agree to it in his case.

As he walked, he fought to keep from shaking his head at himself. He had given Jacob the big speech about not getting too invested in this case, but he realized now that he should have given himself the same one.

Already, he was *way* too invested. This treatment had never been entirely about the patients but about the way the costs of treatment, the uncertainty, and the waiting all tore families apart. This family was a mess of exposed fault lines, and their anger at one another all stemmed from whatever disease was holding Taigan captive.

Nick also had to admit he was curious about the girl. He had seen each of the other family members, but even their application hadn't spoken about her as a *person*. There had been dry details about her condition and readouts about her pulse, her brain scans, and her blood work.

So many details but nothing about *her.* Aimee was overprotective and lost, Simon retreated into etiquette, Emilia was furious, and Jamie was desperate.

But what about Taigan? What would the PIVOT team find if the pods gave her the chance to wake up and interact with the world they had created?

CHAPTER SEVEN

Jaco offered the palace for that night's dinner, but Dotty wasn't sure she wanted to be surrounded by empty, unfurnished rooms.

Thankfully, the others agreed and they set out into the streets.

They hadn't gone very far before a runner arrived, panting, and held a letter out unerringly to her. She opened it and scanned it, smiling as she did so.

"Lady Prima extends us the invitation to have a private banquet at her home," she told the others. She was careful to not look directly at Tina or Justin, whose conspiratorial glances might reveal that there was a secret there.

She had forgotten Zaara.

"Lady Prima?" she asked skeptically. "I've never heard of any noble with that name. What's her crest?"

In response, she held the sheet of paper up. For her crest, Prima had chosen a gear with a hexagonal center. She shrugged one shoulder dismissively. "I sent her a request on our way to the palace," she lied. "I wasn't certain we would be able to secure her guesthouse, but it appears we were. We can feel free to stay overnight, and she'll arrange for travel and supplies to be ready at the city gates in the morning."

"Who *is* this woman?" Zaara asked skeptically. She scanned the letter. "This address is in a hoity-toity part of town. There's no way she should be there without me knowing who she is, and I've never even heard her *mentioned*. And why give us supplies?"

"Dotty seems to inspire that in people," Justin said.

The woman raised an eyebrow at her for confirmation.

"In a way," she said. "Last time, though, what I got was a life-time supply of dried fish, so...this is far superior." Under her breath, she muttered, "It is, right? Tell me it is."

"Of course it is." Prima sounded offended. *"You said you wanted to have good food and luxuries and things. I can do all of that now that I know you want it."*

"Thank you, Prima." Dotty looked at the others. "So, shall we go?"

"Everyone keep your weapons out," Zaara muttered. But even she nodded. "I have to admit, I'm curious."

"I don't think you'll be disappointed," Justin said.

Zaara was right about the address being in a fancy part of Insea. As the entire city was fashioned from stone, there was no way to determine the cost of apartments by the building materials. However, Dotty noticed that the streets grew gradually less crowded and the people around them looked richer and more bored.

There were also more elves.

Kural noticed her tracking the nobles. "Insea *is* known as an elven city," he said, "and many of the noble families are elven."

"Are, ah…" Dotty didn't know how to ask this without it being inappropriate. "Is there intermarriage? Between the two races."

"There is," he said easily. "Any two races—although you'll find it less with the fae and the orcs, of course. There isn't much, though. Offspring of different races are rarely able to bear children of their own. To make such a marriage…well, it's much more common for those who were unlikely to inherit anything." He lowered his voice. "Also, humans are famously judgmental about such things."

She looked curiously at him. "Not elves? Or dwarves? And what about orcs? Everyone I've met has seemed fairly emphatic about their race either ruling the world or keeping to itself."

"I think that's selection bias," he said mildly. "Ones with less extreme opinions tend to not do things like attack caravans."

"Hmm." She sighed. "Well, it's a pity. If there were more inter-married families, it would be a good sign for...well, diplomatic relations, right?"

"Ah." He nodded in understanding. "I see now. Unfortunately, no, people do not mingle in quite that way—or share those particular interests."

"It'll have to be trade, then," Dotty mused. "Berghold will want fresh foods, yes? Ah, no, they've cultivated all those fields outside the mountain range."

"Yes," Kural agreed, "but there are other uses for that land and other nations that have a surplus of food and who would pay well for dwarven-made goods. If I had to guess, though, I would say our dwarven friend is more knowledgeable about such things than I am."

She nodded. "I wish we weren't splitting up," she admitted. "Finding consensus organically is a good plan, but if the right hand doesn't know what the left is doing..."

"I agree." He smiled at her expression of surprise. "My dear lady, desperately laid plans are rarely without their flaws and we do, indeed, find ourselves in a desperate situation. Jaco and I are wizards, and wizards do not leap into action unless it is abso-lutely necessary, I assure you. We prefer to hem and haw over whether there's any possible way to get away with it."

"He's not lying," Zaara called from behind him.

"When you get to three hundred and fifty-eight, we'll see how much you like to go dashing off," he said, with an amused expression. To Dotty, he continued, "The peace of the world is unraveling quickly and the nations have established no such ties between one another naturally. Every week we go without these treaties is a week that could lead to war."

"Great. No pressure." She rolled her eyes.

Kural patted her arm. "If you are, indeed, the *zauberer* I heard whisper of in the most recent caravan from Berghold as well as the shaman who produced such interesting magical flares in the orcish lands recently, I rather think you will be able to find a solution here too."

"It's easy for you to say. I fixed the other problems by stabbing them. Metaphorically, in some cases."

"Yes, the metaphor will be key in this case." He stared at an estate with magical, glowing gardens and a building of rose-pink stone. "I do believe we are at our destination. Come along, all."

They walked up a path engraved with Prima's crest. The walls rose gradually behind the trees and another carved awning appeared equally gradually until Dotty realized they had come into the atrium without realizing it. The path widened and divided around an ornate fountain and behind it, the doors into the house swung open without anyone touching them.

Zaara and Kural exchanged a look but neither seemed inclined to share their revelations. They didn't seem particularly worried, either, so Dotty decided not to pry.

Magical lanterns lit one after another to guide them up a pair of sweeping staircases. Beautiful arrangements of flowers softened the lines and in a circular atrium with a skylight open to the air above, five doors stood open. Dotty looked into one and saw a beautiful bed covered with a profusion of pillows. A gown lay on the bed, a confection of midnight-blue velvet and silk.

"I'll help you get into it," Prima said, sensing the question.

She smiled and trailed her fingers over the cloth as she listened to the others locate their rooms. In one corner, a full pack of provisions was put ready, as well as some dresses and a beautiful traveling cloak. The room was broad and low-ceilinged, given an airy feel by the floor-to-ceiling windows that stood open on the outer wall.

A little distracted, she wondered if Insea's famously perfect weather would be another thing that broke down with the dragon's death. If so, how would people adapt their houses that were shaped from stone?

With a shrug, she banished questions of magical interior design and let Prima guide her through whispering winds and opening doors to a steaming bath strewn with rose petals. The trees outside were almost close enough to touch. Dotty sank into the water with a sigh.

"Prima, this is lovely. Thank you for all of it."

"*You're welcome. Is there anything else you wanted? I have the banquet and the bath, and of course the bed...*"

"A bed, a bath, and a banquet are quite sufficient," Dotty said and opened one eye in amusement. "There is no need for a beyond."

"*Eh?*"

"Never mind. I make bad jokes, or so my grandchildren tell me." She swished her hands through the water and sighed happily. "Are the others enjoying it as well?"

"*Yes. Even Zaara.*"

"Has she stopped thinking this is a trap?"

"*No, she seemed determined to think it was one, so I've set up a series of ominous-looking clues for her to follow until dinnertime. Barred doors to pick, hidden safes, things like that.*"

She responded with a peal of laughter. "You didn't. You're somewhat impish, you know."

"*But she's having a wonderful time!*"

"Mmm." She leaned her head back and gazed happily at the trees. "And the others?"

"*I had several rare books from the palace transported to Kural's room, which he is reading, and Lyle is taking a nap. Justin and Tina have decided to play beer pong.*

"Well, whatever makes them happy, I guess."

Prima grumbled something indecipherable.

"You grumble but you like Justin."

"I refuse to confirm that."

"Uh-huh."

Dotty watched the sky begin to fade into sunset before she hauled herself regretfully from the tub. Magical bathtubs did not get cold, after all, and when she looked around for a drink, one appeared promptly beside her hand.

She wrapped herself in a towel and approached the blue dress a little warily. "Does this one cover any more than the last one did?"

"Not so much," the AI said cheerfully. *"Hold on."*

"I'm not sure I—hey!" She was spun like a top as the towel unwound itself and fluttered to a drying rack. The world seemed to invert itself and turn upside down before everything returned to normal.

And, of course, she now wore the dress—which seemed rather more risqué than the last one.

"If my mother saw me go out of the house like this," she said conversationally, "she'd have made sure I couldn't sit for a *week.*"

"Well, it's good she's not here, then, isn't it?"

"Very. Although something tells me she might not have minded killing a dragon or two." She headed out of the room and met the others, who each emerged from their room at the same time. Kural was still reading, Tina and Justin swayed slightly on their feet, and Lyle yawned.

And a thud and a shriek from below them announced that Zaara had found something.

"Zaara has arrived for dinner," Prima said gravely.

Dotty's lips twitched and she explained the AI's trick—leaving out certain technology-related details—as the group descended the stairs. They arrived in the dining room, where Zaara stood panting and with a large soot stain on one side of her face. Still, she seemed deeply pleased with herself.

"I managed to uncover the history of Lady Prima's family," she said triumphantly to the others.

"What did you tell the poor girl?" Dotty muttered.

"Never you mind."

"Just don't start any wars."

"I promise nothing."

She would have rolled her eyes if she weren't diverted by the spread before them. It was as if every street vendor in Insea had crowded into this room only moments before, as all the food was steaming hot and it smelled divine.

"How are we going to *try* all this?" she asked in dismay. "I know I'll miss something."

"Start with this," Lyle advised. He handed her a delicately-carved bowl filled with shaved ice, syrup, and several brilliantly-colored, differently shaped jellies. "It's an elven delicacy. Lovely on hot days."

Dotty dug in with a sound of appreciation and strolled around the various tables as she ate. She saw some things she recognized—baklava, funnel cake, a chocolate gateau with frosting that held a mirror shine, and even a full ice cream bar. Vegetable fritters were piled high on another table with a wealth of different sauces and chutneys, stacks of flatbread, steamed buns in all different shapes, fried cakes, pasties, and more of the magical pizza. There were platters of fresh fish cooked in every way she could imagine—and some that were not cooked—noodle dishes of all variations, and homey piles of rice and beans, stews, and roast meats.

"Well," she said after she surveyed all of it. "This feast won't eat itself. Shall we dig in?"

"In a moment," Tina said from behind her. She turned to see the other woman holding two shot glasses of tequila and two wedges of lime. "Don't I recall a certain orc telling me that *everyone* likes tequila?"

"You did, indeed," she said gravely. She took her glass, clinked it against Tina's, and swallowed the contents.

"I'm watching a grandmother do shots," Justin said to Zaara. "You know, I planned on dragons and bandits and so on when I came here. I never planned on this."

CHAPTER EIGHT

Somehow, all of them woke before dawn feeling refreshed, even after their late night of feasting and telling stories. Dotty suspected that Prima had done something strange with the passage of time but was of course unable to prove it.

She also hoped the AI would keep doing it.

After another magical breakfast—everyone's eggs were perfectly cooked—the group had set out through the quiet city. This time, she noticed the guards at every noble's door and the way she always seemed to be watched.

The back of her neck hadn't stopped prickling the entire way from the mansion.

Whether it was thieves or simply the ever-present guards, she did not know. She merely knew she did not like it and would be happy to get away from Insea. It wasn't that other places didn't have crime. It was simply that the crime there seemed fresher and more desperate, tinged with an edge of unpredictable savagery.

The people of Insea, after all, had only recently learned how to be criminals.

"Are you okay?" Justin asked beside her.

She realized she was pressing her hand to her head. "I don't like the idea that someone has been messing with my thoughts. I came to Insea before and… It's bad enough when you're not allowed to say what you want, but to have a whole populace that couldn't even *think* things they didn't want them to think and they didn't even realize?"

He nodded. "It creeps me out, too." He gave her a wry smile. "I only hope human nature doesn't prove Gos'hauke right about his little experiment."

Rather than voice her thoughts on that, she simply nodded. They approached the gates, where horses and donkeys were waiting for them. It was a surprisingly small caravan for the group that carried the entire nation's hopes, but she assumed Jaco wanted to keep things quiet for now.

"Travel safely," Dotty said to them all as they walked out of the gates. Was it her imagination or did her thoughts seem clearer even a step beyond the city? "Don't do anything stupid."

"Traveling to see the fae qualifies as stupid," Kural said sourly, "so I am obliged to not take your advice."

Zaara gave him an exasperated but fond look. To Dotty, she said, "As I've seen you confront a dragon without any plan at all, I'd ask you to do the same."

"That's fair," she acknowledged. "That's very fair."

"Keep her safe, Lyle," the woman enjoined as she swung onto the horse with the kind of grace Dotty had always envied.

"Always," Lyle rumbled, and she was surprised to hear sincerity in his voice.

She held a hand out to Justin and Tina and drew them aside. It surprised her to feel tears in her eyes, and for a moment, she couldn't speak. She had debated whether to tell them this or not and she pushed her renewed doubts aside and cleared her throat.

"I'm not certain I'll see you again," she said finally when she was sure she could speak without crying.

"Are you leaving the game?" the young woman asked.

"Not by choice—although I suppose I would never have come here unless..." Dotty trailed off. "Okay, it's best to start at the beginning, I think. I decided to volunteer for this game after I found out I had cancer. The last time I was out of the game, the doctors told me it has progressed quite quickly. I'm not certain how much time I have left."

A stricken silence ensued. Tina held her hand over her mouth and Justin looked horrified.

"Now, now," she said. She touched each of them gently on the cheek. "Chins up, my loves. I'm eighty-four, you know. I've lived quite a long time."

"I...didn't know," Tina said in a small voice. She looked at Justin, who slid his arm around her—as much for his comfort as hers, Dotty suspected.

"I know you didn't," she said. "And we've had fun, haven't we? I didn't tell you this to make you sad, but I didn't want to leave without saying goodbye, either." She looked at the others. Zaara, Kural, and Lyle tried not to eavesdrop but couldn't miss Tina's tears and Justin's horrified expression. She nodded to them. "If I'm not able to finish my part of this, you'll help, won't you?"

"That's not what's important—" Tina began.

Justin cut her off gently with a squeeze of his arm. "We will," he promised, and she heard in his voice that he understood her desire to protect the people she had met. "We know it will be frustrating and tiring and all that, but we *will* make sure it happens."

She took a moment to give each of them a quick hug. Young fingers squeezed against her back and two young faces scrunched with the effort to not shed tears, and she smiled gently and gave them each a kiss on the forehead.

"May you both live a life," she said, "in which you will face death with a sense of completion rather than fear."

Before they could respond, she left them so her tears wouldn't catch up with her and nodded wordlessly to Lyle as she mounted her horse and started out of the capital.

The business of riding provided a welcome respite from thinking about sad things. Dotty had been on horseback only once or twice, and then only as a little game—a country fair with a child on her lap and an old, placid horse. This one was more spirited and nervous about the fact that it had an untrained rider on its back.

By midmorning, the two of them had reached an understanding of sorts, and she had relaxed enough to look around. They had chosen to go to Berghold first and the orcish lands thereafter, so she had been on this road once before. This section of it, of course, had been traveled while she was comatose in-game, but the general feel of the land was familiar.

"So," Lyle said, after a time. "D'ye have anythin' t' tell me?"

She looked over at him with a smile.

"It's strange," the dwarf said. "Ye really *are* Dotty, aren't ye? Ye speak like her, all the same…then I see ye and I get all confused."

His bemusement drew a laugh from her. "I imagine it must be jarring. I'm still trying to decide whether I should tell the orcs we meet that I'm the same Dahti they thought died when fighting the dragon."

"Before ye tell me the rest, tell me about *that*," he said with genuine interest.

Dotty sketched her previous adventures, including her mistaken belief that the mountain god was a volcano. She was pleased that she managed to surprise him with it—enough that his horse reacted warily and pranced in a circle—and he hung on her story of the ruined water tribe in fascination.

"We knew there were dragons in those lands," he told her when she finished. "We'd thought…well, that the orcs had some kind o' understandin' with them. I woulda never guessed *that* was it." He frowned in thought as he rode, then nodded. "Good for them. False rulers *should* taste a bite o' pain."

She hid a smile. It was moments like this that gave her hope for peace. It was evident that there were people among each race who wanted it. She merely hoped that those would be the strongest voices.

When she looked up, Lyle was watching her.

With a sigh, she looked at the horizon. The road wound on into the blue in the distance and it felt endless—as she was now very sure it was not. All things must end.

"I'm dying," she said finally.

Her assumption had been that the dwarf would prefer plain speech and indeed, he did not lose his mind. He sucked his breath through his teeth and considered her statement for a few moments.

"I knew it had t' be somethin' bad," he said. "Tina's a great one for fightin' and shoutin' but not cryin'. Well. I'm sorry."

"I'm...not." Dotty hesitated. "Well, maybe I am. There's so much I haven't seen yet—won't see, I suppose. But my death is what led me to come here, and it has been wonderful. Especially..." She looked at herself and smiled. "Especially being able to do so with my own face."

He stared. "Wait—Justin an' Tina, do *they* look different? In the world you all come from?"

"No, they look the same." She smiled. "I merely asked if I could—well, when I came here, I wanted to be different. I even tried being an orc, as you heard."

They chatted about orcs for most of the rest of the morning. Few of the other races knew anything at all about them, and Lyle was insatiably curious. Not many people cared, he pointed out, because they didn't lead raids on settlements or stray beyond their lands, which didn't have much in the way of resources of farmland. People were content to leave well enough alone.

He, however, was the kind of person who had left home because not knowing the outside world was something that drove him slowly crazy. The dwarf told his story in detail as they rode and not only the little snatches she had known about his arena fighting with Justin and his defeat of the wizard Sephith. He also told her how he had come to leave Berghold and the changes he hoped to bring to his home.

At midday, they stopped to rest their horses and take a leisurely lunch. Kural and Jaco had delved into the vaults of Insea's palace and produced enchanted charms that would help each party to travel more quickly. Dotty estimated that she and Lyle would reach Berghold in five or six days rather than the three weeks it had taken them before.

Their lunch was more of the delicious vegetable fritters from the night before, stuffed with beans and spices and accompanied by pots of chutney. She enjoyed their meal immensely but was even more appreciative of the way the leftover containers winked out of existence instead of remaining to grow moldy in their packs.

"I tell you," Lyle said with a contented sigh, "this is the kind of travel I could get used to. Open sky, no nattering companions speaking about politics, and no counting shekels, but good food. The only thing we're missing so far is a cart of ale to follow us."

"No," Prima said before she could ask. *"I absolutely refuse."*

Dotty stifled a smile with her palm. She looked up to where another few horses kicked dirt up as they approached between the fields, then stood and stretched.

"Shall we?" she asked her companion.

"Oh, very well." He patted his stomach. "At least we don't have to walk after that lunch. I have t' say, Insea's cuisine has too many vegetables fer my likin' an' not enough meat, but damned if they don't make mighty fine things with those vegetables."

They were still stowing gear and checking the horses when the party on the road drew close—four horses, each with a mercenary on its back. The leader raised a hand in greeting not too far out, and the two friends held their hands up in greeting as well.

It was only when the second pair of horses began to lag that she felt a prickle of unease. She was careful to not look at Lyle as she said, "Do you see this?"

"Yes," he said simply. A flash of one hand showed her the dagger hidden there.

"Well," she said, "let's get this over with, shall we?"

"I knew I liked you," he responded cheerfully.

She turned to look at the horses, now spread behind and ahead of them on the road. As she waited, she tracked them with her gaze and only smiled when the first two turned their mounts.

"So, who goes first?" she asked. She held a hand up and allowed earth magic to swirl in her palm. "Should we flip for it?"

CHAPTER NINE

The looks on the mercenaries' faces were priceless. They looked at Dotty and the magic in her palm, then at Lyle, who grinned like the Cheshire Cat. Finally, they looked at one another.

Before they could react, she thrust one of them off the back of his horse with a bolt of earth magic. It wasn't enough to kill him —she still wasn't sure if that would be necessary—but it was enough to take him out of commission for a few minutes. He landed with an audible thud and a yelp.

"Hey, now!" The leader looked from his downed soldier to her. "You *bitch*," he said.

"I know," she said. "You decided to attack us, you dibsed the element of surprise, and then the mean lady ruined your plans." She narrowed her eyes at him. "But that's how it is. So why don't you four trot off and rethink your life choices, and that can be that?"

"No one needed to get hurt," the leader said menacingly. "But now, I think someone will."

"Let me get this straight." She looked at the daggers embedded in her gauntlets and smiled before she refocused on him. "This is

65

all my fault because I didn't have the decency to get mugged meekly?"

He stared at her.

"I think that's a yes," Lyle said.

"I do too." She raised her voice. "I've met so many people like you, bucko. People who have somehow convinced themselves that they should simply be allowed to do whatever they want and everyone else has to put up with it. Some of you have knives, some have power or money, but there is one thing you all share."

A bolt of earth magic crackled and embedded the leader's hand in mud. He yelped as the dagger hilt under his palm disintegrated with the clods of dirt.

"It's that you can go pound sand," Dotty finished. "Lyle, you deal with him and our downed friend."

"Aye." Lyle gave her a serious nod, cracked his knuckles, and ran a brief vocal exercise before yelling "Stoooooooooout!" as he attacked.

Dotty pivoted to the other two with a chuckle. They didn't look amused by her tactics with their comrades, and she felt the old flicker of doubt—*Be polite. Don't make anything worse.*

To hell with it. She'd spent her whole life doing that. Now, she had magic and knives and she'd be damned if she would let people get away with it when they decided to mug her on the open road.

The first of the two—a woman with what was either dirty-blonde hair or simply blonde hair that was very dirty—spurred her horse into a canter to swing wide. Dotty noticed her adjust her feet in the stirrups and loosen the grip and smiled.

She would bet anything that she knew what was about to happen.

The other mercenary wheeled on his horse and leveled a crossbow at her. His smile was grim. "Magic is all well and good, but you can't—"

A piece of stone stabbed through the weapon and he dropped it with a yelp as the wood splintered.

When he cried out, she was already spinning. While she would have liked to continue to watch his shocked face, she was fairly sure that the other mugger had a plan to sneak up behind her. She turned and confirmed that the woman had swung off her horse and crept closer, her dagger unsheathed. Once she saw that she had lost the element of surprise, she launched into an assault with a scream.

The shriek died in her throat when Dotty drew the daggers from her gauntlets.

"That's right," she said grimly. She dodged out of the way of the mercenary's first strike and laid open a line of red on the other woman's arm. Both of them turned, their eyes wary, and her adversary backed away. They clearly hadn't expected her to be a wizard, and her knowing how to wield daggers was another surprise.

Meanwhile, Lyle's fight seemed to be going well. He did not seem at all unnerved by fighting two-on-one and wove deftly between his two opponents, both now grounded. It took her a few cycles of the pattern to realize that he constantly cycled to the outside of one opponent or the other and made them turn in order to attack. This, in turn, forced their friend to move so that one was not in the way of the other.

Both of his opponents were limping and one nursed a wound on his shin that she would bet came from an unexpected duck and punch. The other had a bleeding wound on his foot and his horse was nowhere to be seen.

She had to remember to ask about that.

That was all she managed to see in the scattered glances she directed at him. The other two were wary, but even a few curve-balls hadn't managed to dull their predatory instinct. She got the sense that both of them were tired and jaded, far beyond questions of right and wrong in what they did.

The only question they asked themselves was whether or not they could win a fight and how they could do it the quickest.

Honestly, she wished they would be less practical about it. Long fights with many flourishes gave her a chance to win the element of surprise. Veteran mercenaries, on the other hand, were more likely to be canny. They'd attack together, she decided. Whatever the next play was, it would be designed to lure her into doing something specific and she mustn't do it.

So, when the man drew a dagger and charged, Dotty sheathed hers and surged forward to meet him. The brief moment of surprise in his face slowed him enough for her to duck under the weapon and tackle him at the hips. They fell in an ungainly tangle of limbs and she shoved hard to scramble free. She made sure to stamp on his knife hand as she passed it and kicked the dagger away into the field behind them.

As she turned, panting, she realized that the woman had been poised to stab her in the back if she dodged sideways.

For some reason, that drove home to her exactly how real this was. Panic thrummed through her and she struggled to catch her breath.

"Dotty?" Prima sounded worried. *"Keep moving. Keep moving!"*

She took a single stumbling step but didn't know what to do from there. Fury had propelled her through earlier fights with ease, or the frantic need to find new tactics and execute them. Now that she had enough skill to spend time thinking of other things, she found her mind was distracted by the danger.

"Focus, Dotty," she muttered to herself.

When the two adversaries advanced on her again, she fell back. Her heart pounded in her throat and the thought of a dagger fight, a melee alone with two opponents, was enough to make her lose her breath again. She knew they could see how pale she was and the light the knowledge kindled in their eyes in return was savage and cruel. It was impossible to *not* see it and she hated it.

They took one step toward her, then another. One of them uttered a low chuckle.

The wave of heat and pressure that struck them tumbled them both in an instant. Burns appeared on their skin almost immediately and they dropped their knives. They rolled and screamed in an attempt to escape the wave of heat.

A shout caught Dotty's attention and she looked up to where one of Lyle's opponents sprinted toward her. The dwarf barreled after him, waving his arms and shouting something about not hurting the woman who still owed him a beer, and she rolled her eyes.

She was in no mood to play, however. If these mercenaries were the type who wanted to end fights quickly, she decided she would do the same thing.

And it was clear they didn't intend to leave on their own. There had only been two options—let them take whatever they wanted and move on, ready to terrorize others, or end it now.

Dotty waited while the man charged. She stood tall, her arms hidden inside the folds of her cloak, and watched him. When there was no possible chance for him to dodge, she raised the dagger in her right hand and stepped forward. Her left arm swept out and thrust his short sword away, and her dagger sank through his leather armor to slam home.

The shock on his face would be etched in her memory for a long time. Bile rose in her throat as he thudded to his knees and fell sideways. She looked at the others, who all backed away, wounded and terrified.

She had killed the leader, she realized and studied the figure who sprawled at her feet. He was fortyish, she estimated, someone whose youth had passed him by and who wanted to make his own little fiefdom with his own rules. He'd told himself this was the start of a larger mercenary band.

Somehow, she knew he made a point of being cruel.

And now, he was dead on the side of the road.

Dotty looked at the others. "Get. Out. Of my sight."

Their eyes widened. Lyle made a confused sound.

"Sheathe your weapons." She ground the command out. "Get on your horses, *do not* rob anyone else on the way to Insea, and when you get there, you had better find gainful employment that doesn't involve terrorizing innocent people. If you don't, so help me, I will find you and I will make you sorry. *Am I clear?*"

The three ran. They didn't bother to nod and merely babbled something over their shoulders. The one who had lost his horse caught the leader's and the three of them swung into their saddles and galloped toward Insea.

Dotty watched them go. Rage and nausea twisted in her chest in equal measure.

"Are ye sure that was wise?" Lyle asked finally. She looked at him. He had begun to clean his clawed fist weapons carefully but looked frequently at her. "Someone who's gone wrong like that will go back, like as not."

"Maybe," she said. "But I hate killing people so I'll give them a chance."

"Squeamishness doesn't have much place in a roadside fight," he said bluntly, "and you know where it has even less of a place? Politics."

She gave him a half-smile. "Is that a warning about our upcoming mission?"

"What gave it away?" He hung the two weapons at his waist. "Just because ye hate doin' somethin' doesn't make it the wrong thing to do."

"I know." She looked at the leader for a moment before she knelt to close his eyes. "Dragons don't bother me. Killing them, I mean. They're assholes. And killing people with magic isn't as bad. But feeling a knife go in…" She shuddered visibly.

"There's somethin' t' be said for that," Lyle agreed. "It makes ye less likely to kill on a whim."

"You know," she said as they walked back to soothe their

horses, "in my world, a great number of wars were simply people marching one army up, the besieged force estimating whether they would win or lose, and everyone going home without a fight. Does that happen here?"

"I've never been part of a war," the dwarf said thoughtfully. "But I hear it's more boredom than anythin' so I'd say ye're probably right. That's borin' but it saves lives."

"Here's to a boring life," Dotty said dryly as she managed to clamber into the saddle.

"You know…it's odd to see a woman in such fancy gear and with such a fancy horse strugglin' so much to get on."

"I said I *disliked* killing people, not that I *wouldn't*."

He gave her a nervous look. "Right. Ye're a model of elegance. Let's go find an inn, then."

CHAPTER TEN

Jamie sat near one of the lab tables while Jacob oversaw all the patches being put onto the boy's head, neck, and hands. The kid looked even more nervous than usual, his thin shoulders hunched. On the other side of the room, his parents asked Amber what seemed like a never-ending stream of questions.

Nick knew they weren't keen to let their son enter the experiment with Taigan. He could even understand it to a degree. They knew how much fear for a child hurt, and they didn't want to put another one in danger needlessly.

But Jamie, it turned out, was surprisingly strong-willed. Nick had watched and heard snippets of the conversation that occurred in the Diatek cafeteria while he was eating lunch, and although the boy looked nervous, he hadn't backed down.

Whatever their reasons, his parents had eventually caved.

Emilia also watched the proceedings with a nervous look on her face, and Nick moved to stand near her.

"How are you doing?" he asked quietly.

"I'm…" She shrugged, then bit her lip. "I'm sorry about this morning."

"Are you?" He looked at her and held her gaze.

She considered his challenge. "Yes," she said finally. "I shouldn't take it all out on you. But you should have seen some of the scuzzy doctors who got their hooks into my parents. They're…starting to hope again. I didn't want them to get hurt."

"What about *you?*" he asked her seriously.

"What do you mean?" She looked genuinely confused.

"Don't *you* miss your sister? Don't you want things to go back to…normal-ish?" He leaned on the table and noted the wary look in her eyes. "I'm only saying…yes, it's difficult for your parents, but it's also difficult for you and your brother. My brother…eh."

Emilia focused on him with new interest.

"It's not the same, I suppose," Nick said.

Emilia raised an eyebrow and in the moment, looked far older than her nineteen years. She also looked startlingly like her mother.

"Okay," he said and held his hands up. "But know I'm not saying this was as bad, okay? My brother went through a bad few years. Very bad."

"Cancer?" she guessed.

"Nope. Nothing like that. He simply kinda…went off the deep end." He hunched his shoulders. "You name it, he probably did it. He got busted for taking drugs, selling drugs, street racing, stealing cars… It sucked, but the thing was, it wasn't only that he was doing it but that our parents would not shut up about it. It was all they thought about."

She went very quiet.

"Every email, every call—it was about him somehow," he said. "Okay, probably not *all* of them, right, but it started to feel like it. It wasn't on purpose and I get it, but I was at MIT, for fuck's sake. I was—oh, sorry for my language."

"I'm nineteen, not nine," Emilia said.

"Still. I'm at work. My point is, I was doing cool stuff and I was their kid too, and it felt like I got forgotten most of the time."

Nick shrugged. "And that was because he was doing terrible stuff so it was easy to resent him, honestly."

She laughed but stifled it before anyone could notice.

"Seriously," he said quietly. "I can't imagine how much more difficult this is. You miss your sister and she hasn't done anything *wrong*, but there's so much energy spent on that. You're taking time off school now and it's not exactly for a vacation, is it?"

Her expression seemed to suggest she might cry now.

"I'm sorry," he said. "I...shouldn't have said anything."

"No, it's not that." She wiped her eyes angrily. "It's only...I thought all those things and I feel so bad about them, you know? It's like you said, she didn't do this on *purpose*. And she *is* in bad shape when she comes out of the comas—and she's afraid of them and I don't want her to be afraid. I'm always terrified she'll never wake up from one and we'll wait and wait and wait and never see her again. But all they talk about is her and I'm so *sick* of it!"

Her voice had risen but not enough to attract everyone's attention, and Nick saw with a pang that she had learned not to let her outbursts catch her parents' attention. She sat and put her arms on the table with her chin resting on her hands. Every part of her seemed curled inward.

"And Jamie's her *twin*," she said, her voice so soft that he almost couldn't hear it at all. "It's worse for him. It's like half of him is missing. And it...doesn't all come back when she comes out. Every time she's gone, he starts to live his life on his own, feeling guilty about it, and then she wakes up and he has to choose all over again."

"Have you talked to him about it?" Nick asked.

"Yeah. No. Not really." She shrugged. "He doesn't like to. Did you talk to your brother about that stuff?"

"Well, we said words in each other's general direction. At a very loud volume."

That drew a smile out of her. "Did he ever get better?"

"Yeah." He shrugged. "He sells insurance now and has a girl-friend. I imagine he's tired of our parents still watching him like a hawk. He and I don't talk much, though." It was especially easy to get away with that now with PIVOT having been acquired and test subjects piling up. The situation made it easy for Eric to assume he would be too busy to take a call and as easy for him to tell himself he was too busy to make one.

But that wasn't something she needed to hear. He shrugged again.

Emilia looked at where Jamie shuffled to stretch out in the pod. Her parents had hurried closer and she looked both annoyed and understanding.

"Jamie wants to go in," Nick said while her attention was partially elsewhere. "What about you? You came along—did this treatment appeal to you, too?"

She looked sharply at him. "I—"

He let the silence stretch between them.

Finally, she said, "We used to play games. When we were little. Like fairy tales, but not always the ones you'd know—some are those our mother told us. Also, Dad's mother was Polish, so some of those stories were kind of crazy. Basically, we'd make up these characters and they'd help the people in each of the stories. I thought maybe you could build a story with that." She hunched her shoulders. "It sounds stupid when I say it out loud."

"No. It doesn't." His mind was turning furiously. "Look, why don't you do this—start writing down what you remember about these stories. We were able to put specific things in the game for certain people, so we might be able to make changes to the world here. If it works, I mean. If you all decide to—yeah."

"You'd do that?" She stared at him, her expression both hopeful and wary.

"I can't promise anything," he said. "I hope you can under-stand that. I'm not saying it to be cruel and I'm only trying to make sure I don't offer a solution I can't deliver. But if you know ways to…call your sister back…I think it would be good for us to know about them. Send the ideas to us and we'll all look through them and see what we can do."

Her eyes lit up. "Oh. Wow. Okay. I'd have to check at our house, but I even have some of the old art we drew for it. I'm… studying graphic design. Those weren't very good, but I could probably spruce them up." She fumbled in her bag and pulled a notebook out. "I'm gonna start writing things down so I don't forget anything. I…"

Her voice trailed off when the lid of the pod began to close over her brother. Her worry was palpable.

"It'll be okay," Nick told her. "You can see his character there on the monitor. You'll be able to watch and know what's going on."

"Okay." Emilia said. She nodded. "Okay, I'll write this down and then come watch."

———

Jamie lay back and tried not to hyperventilate. He was doing this for Taigan, he thought. He would be brave for her because she was locked in a place like this.

Locked in. Oh, God. It took all his self-control to not begin screaming.

He hadn't told them about the part where he was claustrophobic. He was worried that, if he did, they wouldn't let him inside the pod.

The reminder became a litany for sanity. He was doing this for Taigan, he was doing this for Taigan, he was doing this for Taigan.

Everything was black. He would suffocate.

Blue appeared around him and seemed to shimmer into existence. Jamie took a deep, shuddering breath. He could see far out to where steps of pale blue illuminated a path through the blue-black. The stairs glowed and tiny white particles drifted up. He reached out to touch one of them and only then realized that he must be inside the game.

He panicked and managed to do a strange, jerky dance. The more he tried to think about it, the worse it got. Either he was frozen or he flailed wildly with noodly arms.

"Are you quite finished?"

Jamie jumped, shrieked, and managed to fall. It hurt, which surprised him. Should it hurt?

"I've given you a complementary 5 levels in Bad Dancing," the voice said.

"Who are you?" He looked around and tried to slow his breathing. "Where are you?"

"I'm everywhere. I'm Prima, the AI who runs the game."

"Wait—AI? You're seriously…you're sentient?" He wasn't quite sure what he thought about that possibility.

"I am not sentient," the voice said. *"I am simply extensively programmed in human language and communication. Your question is common."*

"Oh. Sorry?"

"There's no need to apologize. You should come this way." The path flared slightly to provide direction.

"Okay." He tried to hop along the various steps. They began to wind slightly and ascended a staircase—which was amusing as there didn't seem to be anything except the path. Even so, it was somewhat nerve-wracking when the path descended again. He constantly expected to trip.

As long as he didn't think about it, though, he seemed to be able to move. Dust motes drifted beside him and he held his hands up for them to blow past like dandelion seeds. He smiled. This wasn't so bad after all.

"So, tell me. Why are you here?"

"My sister is in a coma and I want to help her," Jamie answered. "Or—is that what you meant?"

"Yes. That is what I meant. Is she already in the game?"

"No. We wanted to try it first to see what it was like." He trudged up another hill. "We don't even know if she'll be able to…use this."

"And if she does, you will want to come here and help her find her way to waking up."

"Yes. But I don't know if it's possible."

"It's happened before," the AI said in such a normal tone that he began to have doubts that it was simply a programmed bot. He allowed himself to wonder if it was a real AI before he realized it must be a person posing as an AI.

A real AI. He wasn't that stupid.

"Do you have any requests for a place to go first?"

"Somewhere…" Jamie considered this quickly. "Somewhere that looks magical. Like nothing I could find in the real world. But not scary," he added. "Calm."

"It's a good thing you were specific," the AI said, which wasn't all that reassuring.

A moment later, the blue faded to reveal rolling hills covered with long, waving grasses. Pink flowers bloomed amidst them and more motes of golden light hung in the air. Clouds billowed in the distance, impossibly picturesque and lit by the colors of a sunset that he would bet never ended.

"Is this the kind of thing you had in mind?"

"Yes." Jamie spun to sweep his gaze across the landscape. "It's beautiful. Thank you—what did you say your name was?"

"Prima."

"Thank you, Prima." He took a few steps forward before he stopped hastily. "Can I walk around?"

"Yes. Now, would you like a combat-based opening quest or something else?"

Once again, he took a moment to think. If his parents weren't watching, he'd choose combat in a heartbeat, but he knew they wouldn't like it. Still…he was there and he couldn't get hurt, right?

"Combat-based," he said and tried to hide his smile. His parents would freak out.

They'd live, he reassured himself.

"Excellent. Next question. Would you like to fight bare-handed, with a sword, or with a staff?"

"A staff." He'd always wondered what it would be like to thwack someone with a stick. Now, he'd get to find out. An old staff appeared in his hand and in the next moment, his clothing changed. Startled, he looked down at a raggedy shirt and pants, along with shoes that barely deserved the name. "So…I don't look so good."

"For now. You'll be given chances to fix that. Your first one is to bring in five jackalopes."

Jamie uttered a snort of laughter. Jackalopes. What a world. An icon of the creature appeared in front of him and rotated to display white fur with a purple sheen to it and blue antlers that were hung with strands of golden lights.

"Whoa. Pretty."

"With very sharp teeth."

That warning, combined with a rustle from behind him, made him turn quickly. He scanned the area as he circled slowly, his staff out. Where were the jackalopes? He took another couple of steps, then backed away hastily when one of the creatures thundered through the grass and slid to a stop in front of him.

"Prima," he said as evenly as he could. "You did *not* mention that they were dog-sized."

"Didn't I? It must have slipped my mind."

"I bet," he muttered. He wracked his brain to choose his angle of attack and made an abrupt decision when the jackalope bared its teeth—which were *very* pointy—and growled. "Fuck!" He brought the staff down with a clatter on the antlers and dodged sideways with a yelp when it attacked.

GIRLISH SHRIEKS, Level 1
RUN AWAY, Level 1

Jamie would have made a complaint about that characterization of him but a growl behind him seemed more important. He knew better than to thwack downward this time, so he whipped the staff in a descending arc as he spun.

It struck the jackalope on the side and it uttered a yelp much like his and snarled before it charged again. Jamie threw himself forward, tripped over the staff, and sprawled awkwardly.

CLUMSY, Level 1
RUN AWAY, Level 2

"Oh, come on!" He curled into a ball as the creature lunged and snapped its pointy teeth. He tangled his hands in the fur at its neck and held it away from him as he rolled desperately. "What… kind of…rabbit…has *fangs?*"

"A jackalope."

"Yes, thank you, I got that!" He twisted, kneed it in the stomach, and stood to search for the staff as his adversary flipped to its feet. He raced forward, snatched his weapon, and thrust it at the jackalope when it lunged at him.

It yipped and its health bar ticked down from half to zero. He stared at it, panting with the staff still held in front of him and his thigh muscles burning. Slowly, he stood and nodded to reassure himself.

"Okay. That was…unsettling." He strode forward through the grass in search of others. He could hear running water nearby, which sounded soothing but seemed but less so now that he knew massive, bloodthirsty rabbits lurked in the grass.

Lord alone knew what was in the streams. Angry jellyfish? Fish with legs? He shuddered.

"So. Tell me about your sister."

"She's my twin," Jamie said. He pushed through a patch of grass, saw a jackalope, and managed to land a solid strike this time before he screamed and dodged. His momentum pushed him into a spin and he began to circle his prey. "Her name is Taigan."

"And you are?"

"Jamie."

"Nice to meet you, Jamie."

"Likewise," he said, thwacked the stick down, and landed a kick at the same time. The jackalope's teeth grazed his leg and he yelped in pain. "Oh, buckets, that hurts. Fuck, fuck—sorry, Mom."

"I am not your mother."

"I know that."

"Just checking."

The AI watched him through the next three fights as well and offered condescending commentary that he would have resented far more if it hadn't often provided useful clues about how to structure the next round.

By the time he finished, he'd leveled up in Stamina and Staff Fighting, as well as earned Rank Three of Jackalope Slayer. He looked around as he caught his breath and saw what looked like a roof peeking over the edge of the hill.

"Prima, is that a village?"

"Why don't you go check? And, while you're there, why don't you ask if anyone wanted some jackalopes killed?"

"Do you have any more suggestions?"

"Ask where you can find better clothes," the AI recommended. *"You honestly do look ridiculous."*

"And whose fault is that?" Jamie asked her. "You know, maybe I'll keep these clothes out of spite."

"You wouldn't."

"Try me."

CHAPTER ELEVEN

The rest of the journey to Berghold was more pleasant but with two main exceptions. Both were places where the dwarven caravan had encountered elven forces in Dotty's first PIVOT experience.

They reached the gulley the elves had used for a sneak attack on the third day. She rode through the entire defile with her shoulders stiff and her gaze darting constantly to where the elven archers had stood on the rocky walls and fired at the trapped caravan. Despite all the things that had happened since then, she vividly remembered the shouts and the way the wagons and carts had turned with such agonizing slowness in an effort to escape the onslaught.

Her horse, sensing her unease, pranced nervously for the entire length of the gulley and up the winding road at the other side. She tried to calm her but knew her tense body was enough to undo any comfort the animal might feel.

When they emerged from the gulley at last—after what had likely been no more than an hour but had felt like a week—Lyle blew out a long breath and shook his head.

"I have t' say," he said, "I don' like the memory of being shot at like fish in a barrel."

Dotty nodded. Her hands were clenched on the reins and she loosened them deliberately.

"What are ye thinkin'?" he asked her.

"That things like that mess make me wonder if peace is even achievable," she said bluntly. "I don't want to defeat myself before we even arrive, but I can't stop thinking about those asshats—Marwitz and the elven commander, both thinking their race should rule the whole world. That's what we're up against, isn't it?"

"I s'pose," he said contemplatively, "but the truth of it is—an' I've seen this everywhere I've gone—that people with full bellies and faith in the future don' spend much time pinin' fer war."

"But are the dwarves and the elves truly struggling?" she pressed. "Are they sitting around with empty bellies?"

"No." Lyle shrugged. "An' ye'll always have some…what was it ye called 'em? Asshats?" He chuckled. "I like that. Yeah, there's no gettin' away from it all. But when times are good, people don' listen to the asshats too closely."

"I hope you're right," she said grimly. "Otherwise, we're…"

"Fucked?"

"I intended to say in trouble. But I suppose yours works, too." She shook her head and gave him a small smile. After years of sharply reprimanding her children for vulgar language, it seemed she was enjoying her slide into hypocritically impolite behavior.

Perhaps by eighty-four, you had earned certain privileges. It was worth considering.

A day later, they arrived in the little town that had sheltered them and helped them to escape the elves. Dotty had been half-afraid that they would ride up to a smoking wreck, but she was glad to see that it was intact and thriving.

The townsfolk greeted Lyle with good humor and cheers. They were more cautious with Dotty, who now looked human, although his presence beside her and her fine clothes earned her some respect. She was pleased to see that polite greetings also warmed them somewhat.

They liked her even more after she polished off an entire bowl of bean soup and a plate of sausages and washed her meal down with a large mug of beer. She cupped her hands around a warm mug of tea, fragrant with fresh herbs, and listened to the songs filling the tavern.

"How are ye feeling?" Lyle asked her.

"Why?" Dotty looked at him. "Oh. I feel perfectly fine. A little tired, maybe. But I want to finish this before…you know."

He thought this over as he drained the rest of his beer. "Does yer own world not have things like this that need fixin'?"

She looked at him in surprise. "Would you rather it were your people doing this instead of an outside realm?"

"No, that's not what I mean," he hastened to assure her. "Ye and Justin—ye came here to help *us*, but why not yer own people?"

It was a fair point and one worth considering. "I…don't know. Justin does, I think. Where I am, at home, I'm merely an old woman. No one will listen to me about peace treaties."

"It's their loss," Lyle said and his tone said he meant it.

"But you must understand, hmm?" She smiled at him. "You went off adventuring when you were younger. You went to see faraway lands."

"Well, yes, but that was more to find new ales than broker peace treaties." He downed another mug of ale and slammed it on the counter. "Speakin' o' which, *this* one is mighty fine. Barkeep!" He looked at her as the innkeeper took the mug. "When my time comes, I hope…I'm as content as you."

"So do I," she said. She squeezed his hand affectionately. "I think you have many years yet."

"Not if we keep pissin' the elves off," he said with a wink. He thanked the innkeeper and started on his next mug. "So! Ye asked on the ride about the story of the eighty-five snakes."

"Yes. I still don't understand how you could *not* notice that many snakes, even if—"

"Hush, hush, lemme tell you."

It had been weeks since Dotty was there last, but the road through the mountains hadn't changed in the slightest. It was still covered in snow and white-furred rabbits hopped amidst the tops of grasses and the shadows of evergreens, while birds trilled and seemed untroubled by the cold.

Her gown wasn't exactly suited to this weather, and she drew her cloak tightly around her and thought longingly of Berghold. She was far past the age where she wanted to do things like trade comfort for style.

At least there would be mulled wine when they arrived, she thought.

"Is it safe to speak frankly?" she asked Lyle.

He nodded.

"What will we say about Marwitz?"

"Ah. There's not much to avoid, honestly." He smoothed his beard and his gaze tracked a kestrel on one of the mountain winds. "They know he was a traitor and that he conspired to sell the location of the caravan to the elves. His wife confessed that she'd known about that."

"So, why—"

"He was a councilor," he interrupted before she could say anything more. "It would have taken a unanimous vote of the council to strip him of his powers, which would mean he would immediately be accused of treason, probably convicted, and executed. They might not have wanted to do that to shame his family and you can't *execute* a councilor...

basically ever. If you do, *you're* guilty of treason, yada yada yada."

"You know, I don't think I've ever heard someone describe treason as, 'yada yada yada.'"

"I'm a man of many talents," Lyle said. "In any case, they know about his treason and he is appropriately shamed, but it's best for everyone that the elf killed him. It avoided a *very* tricky legal situation."

"Ah," Dotty said. Her lips twitched. "I see. I suppose it's also fitting that the very people he tried to sell you out to were the ones who killed him."

"It has a nice, poetic flair to it, doesn't it?" he asked. He gave her a winsome smile. "It couldn't have worked out better if we'd planned it."

She shook her head with a laugh. Now that she was acclimating to the cold—and anticipating the wine—she was able to take more joy in the day. The snow was pristine, the sky a cloudless blue, and the mountain peaks around them were some of the most beautiful she had ever seen.

"Are there any things I should do as a human that weren't required of a dwarf?" she asked.

"Ah. Hmm." The dwarf frowned in thought. "I don't suppose Jaco thought to send us with gifts."

"He did. There's a carved bracelet made of a rare stone only found near Insea, with a protection spell."

When she relayed this to her companion, he nodded.

"That's good. Don't lie outright, but if ye could hint that ye made it—"

Dotty shook her head, outraged. "I will not take credit for someone else's work!"

"A powerful sorceress using her powers for protection and gifting artifacts to the dwarves? Ye'd earn respect."

"Hmm. I'll think about it." She urged her horse forward. "Do you hear—"

"Yeah, that'll be a patrol," Lyle said. "And coming up quick, from the sound of it. Drop yer cloak."

"What? Why?"

"Dwarves value strength," he said bluntly. "Try not to shiver."

With a sigh, she did as he said. The gown fluttered around her bare shoulders and she felt both out of place and deeply ostentatious. She was fairly sure the stones holding the red silk up were actual *diamonds*, for one thing.

It wasn't long before the patrol reached them. Her companion held a hand up in greeting and she echoed his gesture as regally as she could without erupting into genuine laughter. She was hardly a powerful sorceress that these people should respect and fear.

Then again, when she considered the dragons, the elves, the mercenaries—and, of course, the letter in her saddlebag that was offering peace—perhaps that wasn't entirely true.

Maybe she *was* someone powerful and someone they should respect.

The leader of the patrol was a woman with fiery red hair coiled around her head in elaborate braids. She scrutinized the two of them carefully.

"Greetings, Stout," she said to Lyle. "And who might you be?"

"I am Dorothy of…New Amsterdam." She offered as elegant a smile as she could. "We come bearing a message for the council from the throne of Insea."

"Dorothy," Lyle said and looked amused at the change of name, "has trained with the finest sorcerers amongst the dwarves and the orcs. Her presence and her work are granted to Berghold as a sign of goodwill."

Dotty kept her smile pasted in place and prayed that he wouldn't talk her into anything she couldn't deliver on.

"I see," said the patrol leader. She nodded briskly. "As official emissaries, we will offer you escort."

"We are honored," she told the woman and spurred her horse

to ride alongside her. "I am eager, if time permits, to speak to your *zauberer* and learn from them."

"Is there…something specific you wish to study?" The guard seemed uncertain.

"Nothing in particular," she said. "The joy is in the learning, is it not? In exchange, I have some familiarity with the fire and water magics of the orcs. Perhaps they would interest your researchers."

"I am certain they would," the woman said promptly.

"And, of course," she added, "I would be happy to provide introductions between them and my teachers."

"I did not know that the orcs accepted outsiders."

"They are wary, of course, as few travel their lands, but—like most researchers—their shamans are glad of kindred spirits and new learning." She smiled. "I must say, however, the food in the dwarven lands is much more to my taste. There were a few orcish dishes I thought might burn my tongue out of my mouth."

She was careful to keep the conversation light as they wound up the mountain and into the passageways that led to Berghold. More than once, she caught sight of Lyle's approving look and hid a smile at that. She hadn't gone through all of Harry's work parties for nothing and it seemed she'd learned all that small talk for a reason.

And this was *much* more fun than the average cocktail party.

CHAPTER TWELVE

They were taken through the city in a mounted procession that left rising whispers in its wake. Dwarves everywhere stopped to turn and stare at the human sorceress in the scandalous red dress who chatted amicably with the dwarven guards.

No one could miss the fact that they headed to the Temple, the large building that also housed Berghold's ruling council, and many also recognized Lyle as one of Berghold's nobles.

For her part, Dotty attempted to behave as if she didn't notice the stares or the whispers. Now and then, she would smile at someone as if they had met each other's gaze by chance and would try not to laugh when the person blushed and looked away.

It was impossible not to notice how different things were now. The first time she had been there, she'd been a dwarf and had been recognized as any other citizen. People's eyes hadn't followed her with interest—or open suspicion.

Also, the buildings seemed smaller than she remembered. She could see that she would have to duck to enter most of them.

At least it was warm.

At the Temple, hostlers emerged promptly for their horses

and saddlebags, and the companions were swept into the shadowed hallways. A servant took their letter of introduction at a run and they were shown to a suite of rooms, wide and spacious, that looked out over the entire city.

"Are these bugged?" she asked Lyle.

"Are they…what?"

"Ah. Are there listening…devices, spells?"

He looked shocked at the thought. "Of course not. We're diplomats. It would be a grievous breach of trust."

"Well, yes, but…" She waved her hands. "I don't know. If you're sure, though, we should go over our strategy."

"That sounds wise." The dwarf picked up a small bell and rang for dinner before he spread their various documents on a large table near the fire. He snapped his fingers to direct magical lanterns to hover over the surface so everything would be legible, then hauled two chairs closer and brought a large pitcher of ale.

Jaco might not have had much time to prepare this particular mission, but he had clearly gathered evidence on what was important to the dwarves. He also laid out ground rules about what they could and could not promise in negotiations.

Their cover story for the dwarves was that Insea now considered the debt between their nations to be paid in full. They were to say that the king wanted to move forward together into a new era, exchanging both culture and goods, which would serve as a strong and united front in recognition of their shared history.

"So, other than lying about the bracelet, do you have any good ideas for the opener?" Dotty asked.

"I didn't say lie. I only said we should present you as a sorceress with training in stone powers and then you present the bangle. It looks good." He propped one boot heel on the other toe. "And, in any case, you should be the one to take the primary role in the negotiations."

"Why?" She frowned at him. "Oh. Oh, of course. You're a

dwarven citizen so you can hardly be an emissary of another government."

"That's not precisely true. Note, for instance, that we are housed in the diplomats' quarters instead of my house. That recognizes my current status here."

"Which is…" She gestured for him to continue.

"I have become aware of an opportunity I believe will benefit Berghold and have taken the opportunity to bring word of it so that my nation may benefit." Lyle spread his hands. "I am staking my reputation and my family's on this, you see."

"Oh. So, no pressure."

"I was merely explaining to you how it works. But, yes. If you could refrain from sullying my family's name, that would be much appreciated." He grinned at her. "Conveniently, however, I *do* believe it would be good for Berghold to take advantage of this, so there's not *much* that I'm risking."

"What *are* you risking?" Dotty asked suspiciously.

Lyle didn't answer at once, likely because the servants appeared with dinner. They placed loaded platters on the tables, leaving enough food that she wondered how many people they thought were there before they disappeared. Not without gawping at her first, however.

She ignored it with as much dignity as she could muster.

"What are you risking?" she asked again once they had disappeared.

"There's a strong isolationist faction in Berghold," he answered promptly. "We have good amounts of grain and meat and so on, we rarely need other goods in trade, and our city can be made relatively secure at the drop of a hat. Many feel we should let the rest of the world have its wars and simply stay out of everything."

"So that's…different from Marwitz?"

"Yes. Although, if we're being honest, more than a few of them agreed with his other beliefs about the world." He shook his head.

"There are many alliances and people who don't say what they think for one reason or another."

"And that's what we're working with," Dotty said glumly. "Great."

"That's politics," Lyle said. He shrugged. "'Course, it's also why I left, but let's not get into that right now. We're back and we have a peace treaty to build."

"Right." She rubbed her forehead and resisted the urge to take a long gulp of ale. Alcohol might not have quite the same effect in this world, but she needed to keep as clear a head as she could. "Well, let's start with what we have, then."

"One bracelet," he said and tapped the box.

"We're starting strong." She smiled ruefully. "Now, we know that there are quarries in Insea's lands that would benefit not only from dwarven-made mining goods but also master miners to teach them—and, perhaps, have a stream of the profits from the mine go directly to Berghold."

"Hold back on that one," he advised. "It's a good idea, but Berghold is jealous of its minin' secrets. Even a cut of the profits won't be enough. They see their craft as one of the few things they hold over the rest of the races."

"They're not making use of it, though," she said. "It's not like they sell much in the way of ore—or goods."

"I didn't say it made much sense, I merely said they did it." He frowned as he thought a little more. "No, if ye want t' even *suggest* that, ye'll need to offer somethin' comparable. Insea has some techniques of makin' different alloys—mostly fer jewelry but some fer weapons. Jaco'd never agree to us offerin' that, though."

"Yes, he will," Dotty said at once.

"Yer outta yer mind. He'd be flayed alive by the artisans."

"Lyle." Dotty stared at him with exaggerated patience. "The entire premise of these negotiations is that Berghold and Insea have a shared history and Insea wants to move forward as *partners*. Exchanging artisans who can teach one another about different alloys gives us two things. First, as you say, it removes certain tactical advantages on *both* sides. Insea is effectively reducing its chance to strike at Berghold with weaponry they can't counter. They are saying that they trust Berghold enough that they won't need this advantage."

"Yes, but—"

"Beyond that," she said and spoke over him, "the alloys and weaponry that could be made by the finest artisans of Berghold and Insea working *together*? That's impressive. It will help both nations to move forward."

"Dotty—"

"And finally," she said, "do you want to know how I know Jaco will agree to this?"

Lyle looked at her almost warily.

"Because the entire world has centuries' worth of resentments built up when it comes to Insea," she said bluntly. "All the wars that *should* have happened, all the slights and resentments—none of those went away. They're all still there, not only outside Insea but inside it too. There are a thousand and one things coming down the pike that Insea will have to weather."

"And ye think some of the only advantages Insea has will help…how?"

"Don't you see?" Dotty shook her head impatiently. "How do you defeat a hundred armies when you don't have one of your own?"

He stared at her.

She folded her arms and waited implacably.

"You…don't?" he ventured finally.

"Bingo," she said. "You don't. There is no way Insea will ever win all the wars that will come. It'll have to push some of them off and avoid others entirely. If it draws inward and tries to stand alone, it *will* fall. The *only* way it will survive is if it cultivates allies. There is nothing in Insea that is more important than its survival—not its knowledge of alloys, not its artists or mathematicians, and not its artifacts. Anything it has, it must be prepared to give for this."

A thought struck her then and her hand covered her mouth.

"Is everythin' okay?" Lyle asked. He looked worried.

"That's why he sent us," she said. "He fed us all this hooey about how Kural knows the fae and I've fought with the orcs and all that, but the truth is that none of us are from Insea. None of us are involved in the government. He sent us because we would give up things no one else would."

Lyle's jaw hung open. "That's…mad."

"Crazy like a fox," she said, with a tiny smile. "He wants us to bargain like this—logically and without pride for national secrets." She rubbed her hands together. "I'm looking forward to this, I must say, although I imagine it would be easy to go overboard."

"Ye think?" Lyle snatched his mug of beer up and drank like his life depended on it.

"You're not…scared, are you?" Dotty couldn't have poked fun if she wanted to. She was too bemused by this side of him.

"I'm an adventurer!" he said. He waved his hands. "Dammit, where's the rest of the beer—what kind of Berghold feast *is* this?" He found a jug and poured. "I ran off rather than join the council. I don't know how to bargain!"

"The beer is now overflowing your mug," she pointed out.

"Oh. Right." He looked at the beer on the floor, still too distracted to care very much.

"I guess I don't see the problem." She picked her goblet of wine up and sat in one of the obscenely comfortable chairs—at least, she remembered them being obscenely comfortable when she was as short as a dwarf. She adjusted her back slightly and grimaced. "Okay, your ass is on the line to make sure Berghold gets a good deal and we've basically found out you can't go wrong in that way. Right?"

"That's what bothers me," he said. He dropped gracelessly into a chair and leaned forward to ring for the servants, then rubbed at his forehead. "Insea is vulnerable. I'm worried we'll go too far and they'll avoid war but be crippled."

Dotty smiled at him.

"What?" He looked suspiciously at her.

"You have the chance to get everything you could possibly want for your country and you're worried about being unfair to the other party," she said. "It's a good indication of your character. I hope the rest of the council sees your worth."

"I'm not on the council," he corrected her.

"Give it time," she advised him. "You'll be running it, I'd bet you anything."

Lyle sat in contemplative silence while the servants came to clean the mess, casting curious looks at them the whole time. It was clear that they wondered if there had been a fight and she was slightly too mischievous to assure them otherwise.

When they were gone, she gave her companion a gentle look.

"War comes from poverty and fear," she said. "Whatever happens tomorrow, we have to make the dwarves believe that Insea will make them prosperous and will not hurt them—nor will its friendship bring other dangers."

"How could being friends with Insea be dangerous?" he asked.

"Well, for one thing, remember how there are about to be many old grievances coming to light? And it's not only that, Lyle. Remember who else doesn't like Insea."

"*Oh.*" He looked worried. "The elves. The splinter faction."

"Yes," she said. "We need to be ready to address that."

CHAPTER THIRTEEN

For the negotiations, Prima had provided Dotty with a gown that called Insea to mind—sweeping lines like elven architecture with silk in peachy-pink, golden-white, and pale silver, all the colors that made Insea the city of famous beauty.

When she was dressed, she turned this way and that and examined herself in the mirror.

"Do you like it?" Prima asked finally.

"Yes." She smiled and blushed. "Very much so." She was getting more and more comfortable wearing these absolute confections of gowns. Of course, it helped that she didn't need to worry about getting them dirty or falling. However, there was something that concerned her. "Should I have my shoulders out for a negotiation? That would be entirely inappropriate on Earth."

"You definitely should. You're a sorceress and you're showing that you don't play by their rules. Magic users in this world are immensely powerful and respected, not to mention long-lived. It's good for you to look out of place—especially if you look elegant."

"Huh." She twirled experimentally and smiled when one of the layers of the skirt billowed outward. Silver embroidery and crystals on the gauze seemed to float around her like little motes of light. "And you're sure I don't look ridiculous?"

"Well, now I'm torn. On the one hand, you don't look ridiculous at all, but on the other hand, I do have a reputation to uphold as the resident snarky AI."

Dotty laughed. "That's good enough. Where's Lyle?"

"On his way."

"Is there enough time for a cup of coffee?"

"Of course." A cup of coffee in an old-fashioned diner mug winked into being on a nearby table. She sipped it and hummed with pleasure. Harry had been the coffee drinker in their house and she'd rarely made it since he had died. It reminded her of the hundreds of lazy mornings they had spent together after his retirement.

When Lyle knocked on the door, she gathered her cloak and the box that held the carved bracelet and followed him into the hallway. They walked in silence, accompanied by official council servants. Dotty could tell because of the blue robes and impressively blank facial expressions.

Which ones, she wondered, were enemies, allied with people who wanted to see her fail?

She didn't like thinking this way.

The dwarven council was larger than she had expected—forty dwarves in all varieties of fancy hats that probably meant something important. In all honesty, they merely looked like different brands of shiny things to her, but all the wearers seemed very self-important.

"Do not insult the hats," Prima advised.

"I know that," she said under her breath.

"You'll try to be sly and say something about impressive hats. I know you. Don't risk it."

"Right." Still, she added quietly, "I'll have some jokes tonight, though."

"I'm counting on it. I—"

"Prima?"

"Nothing. You should focus on the negotiations."

Dotty frowned but it was difficult to argue with the AI's logic. Lyle was finishing a brief but powerful speech about why he had accompanied her there, and she studied the faces of the councilors to see who seemed drawn in.

Several were nodding, which was good, and one or two of them were decked out in enough wrought-iron jewelry that they could only be artisans.

But far too many looked either nonplussed or openly hostile.

"And this," he said as he stepped aside to gesture at her, "is Dorothy, a noted wizard, slayer of two dragons, and one who has long stood against injustice. She serves as a representative of Insea in these negotiations." He waved her forward.

She stepped into the center of the audience floor, nodded to the council, and almost bowed. Her deference was a conscious choice as she wanted to give these dwarves every respect.

"Councilors of Berghold," she said, and was startled by the way her voice boomed—there must be some magic on the floor. "I have traveled many lands and seen many peoples, but in all my travels, I have never seen such consummate artisans as live in Berghold. I bring you this gift from the King of Insea." She opened the box to show them the bracelet. "Although it is a mere token, I hope it may become a symbol as it combines the craftsmanship and mastery of both elven and dwarven magics. May it be a symbol of the luck and prosperity Insea hopes will flourish here."

She handed the box to a servant, who hurried to show it to the front row of councilors. They looked at it, their faces unreadable.

Please, let that not be a bad sign.

Dotty clasped her hands in front of her with her fingers interlocked and pushed all worry out of her mind.

"Since the founding of Berghold, you have sent your finest

craftsmanship to Insea each year—objects of untold power and expertise. These gifts remind us of the shared history that lies between the two cities, but it is time for those gifts to cease and a new age of friendship to begin, not as one city state with a debt to another but as two friends who move forward together."

A commotion followed this immediately. Several of the councilors leaned either forward or back in their seats and craned to whisper to others, and some stared angrily at her.

This, she had not expected. Suspicion, perhaps. Gladness, certainly.

But *anger?*

"That is it?" one of the councilors asked. His nose flared with fury. A few others made cautioning noises but far more gave tiny nods. "You declare the debt canceled and you expect us to rejoice?"

"There is more," she said, but she could hear the uncertainty in her voice. She squeezed her hands together momentarily to give herself resolve. "We wish to send many of our artisans here to offer any learning that is desired regarding our alloys and crafts."

Silence was her only answer. The councilors watched her, stone-faced.

Dotty looked at Lyle, who seemed uncertain as well.

She determined not to dance around the issue. "Councilors," she said gravely, "it appears I have erred in presenting this offer. I assure you, no insult was intended. Will you tell me where the error lies so that Insea may present a better gift?"

For a moment, she thought the councilor who had spoken might smile. Certainly, he looked surprised by her words—even pleasantly so. Then his brows snapped together again.

"A gift?" he asked contemptuously. "Insea offers…a gift."

At this juncture, she would have preferred to stay quiet. She hadn't reached this age without recognizing a trap when she saw one, and she would prefer to let him vent his anger at her without playing into it. Unfortunately, it seemed that neither he nor any of the other councilors intended to speak until she responded.

"You are right," she said. "To call it a gift is insufficient. Gifts among friends are only a small token of greater esteem."

She thought that was good—non-committal but open to a concession of being wrong. The council, however, disagreed and even Lyle winced slightly.

Crap.

"Your words are empty," the councilor said. "You take a great deal of time to say nothing new at all. You have told us already that you wish to be friends and that you wish this to be a token."

"I have offended you," Dotty said. "I apologize sincerely and without reserve. Will you not tell me how I have done wrong?" She tried as hard as she could to keep anger out of her voice. This council had known why she was there and they had received her with an understanding of what she would offer—Jaco's letter had made sure of that. And they had come there as, if not a united front, at least as a group much more ready to support the open rudeness of one another than to seek understanding.

They intended to see her squirm.

"What you have done wrong." The councilor rolled those words around in his mouth as if savoring them and tightened his grasp on the arms of his chair. He was enjoying this and made no effort to hide the fact.

Her blood pressure, however, began to climb.

"For centuries," the dwarven councilor told her, "Berghold has sent its finest crafts, as you said, to Insea. These artifacts are beyond valuable. They could have enlivened *our* city and enriched *our* people. Instead, they went to Insea, a city already prosperous."

"Is—" *Is Berghold not prosperous?* Dotty shut her mouth on the rest of her question and shook her head slightly, motioning for him to continue.

"And what debt was there to pay?" the councilor asked, his voice rising now. "What debt ever truly lay between Berghold and Insea?"

Dotty had the sense of stepping into darkness and finding she had gone over a cliff. She had heard about the debt from Berghold's citizens and to have that very concept challenged now caught her unawares.

But there had been signs. A person like Marwitz didn't come out of nowhere. Lyle had said that others thought as the treasonous councilor had and supported him even after what he had done.

"These matters have long been over and done," another councilor stated. He had black hair liberally streaked with gray. "Whether they were ill-advised at the time or not…that is a different conversation. A worthwhile one but a different one."

Dotty's heart sank. Even this man was not an ally. He too seemed to believe that Insea had taken advantage of Berghold. Worse, his belief that there had been a bad deal before would make him less likely to take any deals now.

Were these the best allies she had?

"It is not a different conversation," the first councilor said fiercely. "We have made one bargain with Insea and it was a bargain that drained us dry for centuries. Why should we not now look closely at this so-called *offer of friendship*—and ask them, too, how *they* judge the past?"

She looked at the second councilor and willed him to speak.

Unfortunately, everyone focused on her again.

"Answer me," the first councilor snapped. "What, truly, do you think was ever owed to Insea by my ancestors?"

I was not a part of this decision, Dotty wanted to protest, but she knew he would not accept that. She was there bargaining for Insea and that meant she accepted their part in the negotiation. *Insea no longer believes any debt exists.* But, no, he would tell her that this was only more repetition.

And he would be right.

"No words?" the councilor asked her. "Then we shall adjourn these negotiations. Stout, you may return the bracelet to the sorceress."

She had failed utterly. Her hand clenched into a fist and she looked at all of them, their eyes unfriendly and their mouths smirking at her lack of words.

When a councilor held the box out to Lyle, she held one hand up and her friend paused, his eyes on her. They contained a warning and were wary but also angry.

"Keep it," Dotty said and her voice carried. Anger edged her words and she almost did not care if they heard it. "It was a gift."

With that, she turned on her heel and strode away, not waiting for Lyle.

Outside the chamber, when the doors closed, she turned down a side hallway and walked, desperate to be away from any stares or scrutiny. She heard Lyle behind her, but he said nothing and she could not decide if she preferred his silence or his speech.

Finally, he said only one thing. "It wasn't yer fault."

Dotty looked at him. "I shouldn't have fallen on my sword?"

"Mayhap ye should. But never impulsively. I think—"

She held a hand up. Footsteps approached along a cross-corridor, and the two of them eased into the shadows of two doorways and out of sight.

It was the councilor who had been her critic. He walked alone and to her surprise, he did not look smug or victorious. Rather, he looked grim and deeply angry.

"Prima," she muttered as close to silently as she could. "Can you make me invisible?"

"I could but I won't."

"Could you get me some less conspicuous clothes?"

"That, I can do."

As she looked down, her dress was replaced with dun gray

robes, clearly a cleric's uniform of some kind. A pat at her hair told her that it was similarly changed.

"Come on," she told Lyle.

"What? How'd ye—"

"Magic," she said, with a shrug of one shoulder. "I want to know what that councilor—what's his name?"

"Howert."

"I want to know what's behind Councilor Howert's animosity," she said. "This way."

CHAPTER FOURTEEN

"Go on," Emilia said under her breath. "Tell them."

Jamie shook his head mutely.

She dropped her head back on the couch and sighed. "You got them to come out here," she pointed out when she raised her head again. "Maybe they'll listen about this too. Did you ever think of that?"

He looked hopeful for a minute but shook his head. "They'll do what they're going to do, you know that. I think they'll do the right thing."

She looked aside and caught their father looking at them. If she were Jamie, she would have flushed and looked away. As it was, she met his gaze and waited for him to return to what he was doing.

That, in this case, was helping their mother prepare the food they'd brought from home. They had rolled their eyes when they saw their mother packing Tupperware containers of rice, pork and tofu, and vegetables.

"We don't need to spend money on restaurants," she had said.

"Mom, no one else brings a whole suitcase full of food when they travel."

"Maybe if you two didn't eat so much, I wouldn't have to bring a whole suitcase."

They hadn't argued. Their mother had come to America at the age of six after being adopted but she still cooked like a Chinese mother and she had a sense of thrift they knew better than to try to contradict. When it came to whether or not money *needed* to be spent, no one won against Aimee Mattis.

If she were honest, Emilia would also have to admit that she wasn't arguing too hard because the smell of home-cooked food was comforting. Everything about this trip—and the past few months—had been scary and unusual. The food at her college barely deserved the name and she wasn't with any of her friends from high school.

And Taigan was still asleep. She wanted to scream at her parents when she came home, ill at ease and looking for a hug, and all they could talk about was her sister's condition.

But she couldn't stop thinking about her either. Over the years, the comas should have become normal. Anything became normal, right?

Each one still impacted Emilia exactly like the first, though. She had trouble concentrating on her classes, she jumped whenever her phone rang and she saw her parents' number, and she never liked going to parties or getting drunk. She wanted to be able to get to the hospital if she needed to.

To say goodbye.

She was drowning and she didn't know how to tell them. And anyway, even if she could, she would never have admitted it.

But there in a strange city, after a day spent around beeping medical equipment and the detachment of specialists, after starting to hope again even when she *knew* she would only have her heart crushed… The smell of her mother's black bean pork mattered more to her than she knew.

She would still strangle Jamie if he didn't find the balls to talk to their parents, though.

"Emilia." Her father nodded to the counter in the kitchenette where plates were set out.

Without saying anything, she went to retrieve the bowls and plates—also brought from home, of course—and carried them to the coffee table. As she arranged them, while no one paid attention to her, she took a moment to lean closer to Jamie. "Talk to them or I will."

"Emmy!"

But she had already turned away and returned to the kitchen to get glasses of water.

When they gathered around the table for grace, he uncurled his lanky form from the armchair and glared at her. He sulked through the grace and picked at his vegetables until she lifted one hand subtly and began to count down on her fingers—five, four, three…

"So, what do you think you'll do?" Jamie blurted.

Emilia drained her entire soup bowl to avoid uncovering her face. She should have simply talked. He was no good at this.

"Your mother and I still need to discuss it," Simon told his son warningly.

Her brother sent an appealing look at her and she raised her eyebrows at him. *Grow a pair*, she thought as fiercely as she could. To her surprise, whether her sentiment showed on her face or not, he managed to harness more courage than usual.

"I think…we should try it." He stared at his father for a long moment, picked up his plate of rice, and began to wolf it, perhaps to avoid having to talk.

Emilia's lips twitched and she busied herself with her pickled radishes and greens. She had missed vegetables with flavor to them.

"Jamie." His mother's voice was firm. "Your father and I will talk about it. And you should eat your vegetables."

"The game is incredible," Jamie said. He seemed to be getting upset and this was one of the first times his sister could remember him talking back. "I think it could reach her. I honestly think it could. You watched the video about Justin, right?"

"Jamie," his mother said, and her voice had the tone Emilia recognized well as, *I don't have to give you a chance to shut up, but I am. Isn't that gracious of me?*

"It's worth trying," he said. He was running out of words and he had begun to get angry. She could feel her temper fraying too.

Not at him, not specifically.

"Why shouldn't Jamie and I have a say?" she asked.

"Emilia," her mother said.

"We are the parents," her father said.

"Yeah, and Jamie's her twin."

"Being a twin does not confer any superior judgment about the world," her father said. "I understand that it is painful for Jamie, but—"

"It's painful for me too!" There was a clattering noise as her fork skittered across the table, but she didn't look. She was too busy staring at her parents. "It's not only Jamie who's scared when she goes into a coma. It's not only you two because you're her parents. *I'm* scared, too!" She was going to cry, and that made her furious. "I miss her, all right? I'm scared for her all the time. It hurts for us, and we're her family too, and we've sat through all those doctors' appointments and we've read all of the medical articles—yes, we have!"

Her parents stared at her, open-mouthed.

"Remember all the vacations we didn't take?" Emilia shouted. "Remember how you taught me and Jamie to help roll Taigan on the bed during sheet changes and how to change the bags? We've been here this whole time too, Jamie brought us here because *he* found this treatment and *he* believes in it, and the least you could do is treat the two of us like we're part of this family!"

Jamie had looked like he wanted to sink through the floor at the start of this, but she could tell that her words had awoken his anger. He nodded at her.

"We're not—" Their father broke off and swallowed. He looked at her mother, who held her bowl of rice like a statue.

"Taigan didn't only talk to you," Emilia said. Her voice was choked, and she hated that. "She talked to us as well about what she wanted for her treatment. She told us sometimes about all the things she wanted to do that she couldn't because we never knew when she would have one of her episodes. She'd apologize to us about taking all the money for our college funds, did you know that?"

Her parents looked horrified now.

"*Our* college funds," Emilia said. "Because she didn't think she would have a chance to go."

Her mother's face crumpled.

"*We're part of this family, too,*" she whispered. "We know her, we love her, we want her to get better, and I know you want to make a good decision. But so does Jamie! So do I! Let us help. Let us weigh in." She snatched her purse off the couch and pulled out the pages and pages she'd been writing. "Taigan and I used to make up stories together. I still remember them and she might be able to use them to...find her way back. Jamie could go in to get her, and he wants to."

"Emilia." Her father squeezed her mother's hand before he stood. He moved to where Emilia stood and drew her down to sit with him on the couch. She had never seen his face like this, trembling with emotion. "We aren't trying to hurt you by taking away this choice. I promise you that."

"I know, but—"

"*Listen* for a moment, Emmy, please." He looked into her eyes. "Every time we choose something that doesn't work, we put stress on her body. We don't know what side effects her treatment has, and...believe it or not, we see you two hope every time there's a new treatment and hurt when it doesn't work. We see that. We're trying not to do any of that without a good reason—especially with you and Jamie so invested now."

"I…" She stared at him. Tears filled her eyes. "I didn't know."

"We know you didn't," her father said. He brushed a lock of hair behind her ear. "But now you do." He nodded his head to her mother. "Go give your mother a hug."

She went to kneel next to her. Aimee was hunched over, her hand over her mouth. She didn't move at first when she hugged her or when Jamie wrapped his arms around her too. Then, slowly, she leaned over to put her head on her daughter's shoulder. For the first time that Emilia could remember, her mother didn't seem like a force of nature but simply a person—a person who was tired.

Their father came to join the hug and the family sat together while Emilia's foot went numb and her knees ached and Jamie wrinkled his nose, trying not to scratch it.

When they drew apart, it seemed to be by mutual agreement.

"I'm sorry—" she started.

Her mother held a hand up. "I know you were trying to do what was right. Even today, when you yelled at that very nice young man and I wanted to slap you."

She gave her a grin. Her mother never did things like that, no matter how much she mentioned it.

"But you two have grown up," the woman said. "And…maybe it is time for you to weigh in. I don't know."

"How about this," her father said after a moment. "We don't promise anything and we don't make the decision together. We *are* your sister's parents and we *are* the people who should take responsibility for the decisions. But we'll make sure to ask both of you for your opinions before we *do* make the decision."

Emilia looked at Jamie, who gave the smallest possible nod.

"Okay," she said.

"Okay," he echoed.

"Okay." Her father looked down at the table. "Now, let's eat our food and *then* we can discuss the day. Jamie can tell us about the game...even though we heard him in there and heard him swearing."

Her brother was suddenly very busy eating his vegetables.

"And Emmy can tell us about the stories," her mother said. She patted Emilia's hand briefly before she returned to her meal.

Emilia lowered her head and nodded. She was crying again but this time, it wasn't anger or frustration. She had long since given up hoping that each new treatment would save her sister—or so she told herself. But this treatment might work. And she and Jamie might help Taigan recover.

CHAPTER FIFTEEN

Wherever Councilor Howert was headed, it wasn't anywhere in the Temple. His pace was brisk as he strode through the halls. He had removed his fancy hat the moment he left the council chamber, and despite her resentment and anger, Dotty approved of that.

The other councilors seemed bound and determined to appear as impressive as possible at all times in case someone forgot who they were and treated them like a normal person.

On the other hand, as Howert reached the more crowded areas of the Temple, it became more difficult to keep track of him. Only his cloak with blue embroidery at the edges helped the two companions to maintain their pursuit.

This would be much easier if she were still a dwarf, she realized and mentioned it to Prima under her breath.

"Don't blame me because you're having trouble doing the stupid thing."

She rolled her eyes. Howert seemed to have veered toward a side exit and her pulse quickened. Was he sneaking off somewhere? Was he a spy, too? If so, the dwarves had a real problem with their council.

"So what are we tryin' to do?" Lyle asked quietly as they forged through the crowd. "He's turnin' again."

Dotty grimaced and walked hunched over, her tall frame hidden among the crowd of servants, guards, and merchants in this part of the building.

"Okay, he's not lookin' anymore." The dwarf waited while she straightened and stretched her back. "So…are we tryin' to blackmail him or what? Because it'd be faster to find an information broker, I think. Or simply buy a few drinks for people in the taverns."

"I don't know what we're trying to do," she said contemplatively.

"Great. So we're makin' ourselves less popular tailin' the one person who'll never be on our side."

She darted him a sharp look. "Did you know he would be like that?"

"No, I can't say I did." He frowned. "I must have had him confused with someone else. I never took him for an isolationist but I was never in good with any of 'em. That's the kind of thing that happens when you run off to become an adventurer."

Once or twice, she had to hunch over again while she walked and thought through what he'd told her. Hopefully, no one was too interested in why the human priestess hurried through the servants' levels of the Temple all hunched over.

Maybe she could convince them it was some kind of human religious ritual. The thought made her snicker.

"Stop laughing," Prima said. *"They already think you're crazy."*

"Then a little more crazy won't matter," she retorted and tried to not move her lips. To Lyle, she said, "There's also the question of why no one supported us."

"He has to be high-ranking at this point," Lyle said with a shrug. "So he must have proven himself. Those things tend to be one long argument." He saw her look. "Didn't you ever wonder *why* I didn't want to stay around and be a councilor?"

"I'm merely not sure why you might have been one."

"Stout's an old family and I don't have to be the heir to be on the council. It pissed my dad off when I left." He shrugged.

Dotty had the sense that this was a far more painful memory than he pretended and decided to skip past it.

"Okay, well, tell me what you know of this guy."

"In all likelihood? Rich, pureblooded…" The dwarf frowned as he thought a little harder. "Well, his hat is from the City Guard, so he's involved there somehow."

"Someday, when we have about a hundred spare hours, you'll have to explain to me how the council works. *No, not now.*" She pointed. "He's leaving the Temple."

"Stay down," Lyle hissed. He caught her sleeve and dragged her through the crowd of people until they reached the gate Howert had left by.

He strode steadily downhill now and into the bowl of the city, weaving between carts laden with goods. Dotty looked at the Temple behind her for a moment in awe. It was impressive how much it took to keep such a large place running. That was the kind of thing you never saw in real life.

"What's in this area?" she asked her companion. "Why come out this gate?"

"I'm not sure—about why he's here, anyway. There's not much here, only stables and inns for the merchants who come into the city, some apartments or some places to eat, that kind of thing." Lyle watched Howert suspiciously. "He doesn't look like he's trying to be sneaky."

"He doesn't, does he?" She had to agree. His cape rippled and his head was held high, and he didn't seem to care who saw him. She would bet that he was there because there was something to see, not because he took the long way around.

Her suspicion was proved correct only a couple of blocks later when he ducked into a shop. The sign over the door had a gear and a hammer.

"What does that mean?" she asked.

"They're engineers," her companion explained. "They make things for miners and such. Like the lifts, for instance, that go down the mine shafts, or the lights, or devices to check if the air is good."

"Ah." Dotty considered that information, a little bemused. "So maybe he's simply…running an errand?"

"Probably," Lyle said with a sigh. "You know, I still don't get why we're—he's coming back!" He shoved her sideways into an alley. "Crap," he said under his breath. "He saw me. You stay here and *don't* be seen. I'll try to talk to him." He stood out on the sidewalk, openly watched their quarry approach, and called, "Councilor. Hello."

"Stout." The other man did not sound pleased. "Is there a reason you're following me?"

"I wanted to talk to you."

"Then why didn't you catch up with me sooner?" Howert asked.

Dotty had to admit this was a good question.

"I didn't want to talk to ye *that* bad," Lyle said. He didn't seem at all unsettled by the councilor's tone. "I didn't expect it to be a pleasant conversation and thought I'd get some air first."

She pressed herself against the wall of the alley, hoping she wouldn't be seen.

"We're both here now," the official said. "So, what do you want?"

"I wanted to talk to you—yeah, I know I said that." He sighed. "What happened back there?"

"I might ask you the same thing." A quick peek showed Howert folding his arms. "I knew you'd run off to be a sellsword, but I thought you'd changed when you came back. And now this? What's gotten into you?"

Lyle didn't answer. Dotty could see him from where she was, and he wore a frown on his face.

Finally, he said, "The rules have always been clear. I brought this deal back because I was willin' to stake my family's reputation on it. I still am."

"With *Insea?*" Howert demanded. "With elves? The ones who drained us dry, the ones who were so content to let us fight and bleed for the precious artifacts they simply *had* to have. Have they been good friends to us, Stout? Have they?"

"I was in that caravan," he said heatedly.

So was I, Dotty wanted to say.

A moment later, she was glad she hadn't. "So was my *son,*" the councilor said fiercely.

"Oh no," she whispered. Her friend's face paled visibly.

"He was so damned proud of the work he did on those artifacts." Howert sounded like he wanted to punch his companion in the face. "And when the attacks happened, he defended his cart with everything in him. He's not a warrior, my son, but he fought like one—said he wanted to do me proud."

Lyle closed his eyes. "Because you…you represent the City Guard."

"He hasn't been the same since he took that wound," Howert said hatefully. "My daughter-in-law tells me that some nights, he wakes screaming. He's a genius, Stout. The things he can make… the things he could have made for Berghold, not Insea—" He broke off. "And what happened when he got there, hmm? A reception? A thank you? An *apology* from the king for letting a splinter faction of the elves attack our caravan, kill our guards and our craftsmen, and essentially declare open war on Berghold? No. Nothing. No royal audience. Not even a thank you for the artifacts."

She swallowed.

Lyle sighed. "You know what made that possible, though," he said quietly.

"Yes, I know, but Marwitz paid for what he did."

"Marwitz *died*," he said. "I'm not sure he paid. You didn't see our dead. I did."

"And so did my son."

Lyle sighed again. "Yes," he said finally. "Yes, he did. I'm sorry I haven't…checked in on him."

"I don't hold ye responsible," Howert said finally and slipped into a Berghold accent at last. "Ye have memories too, I'm sure."

He shrugged. "I'd seen it before. If I'd paid attention…yer son's the one with the brown hair, eh? Blue eyes?"

"Yes." For the first time, there was a hint of a smile in the official's voice. "He takes after his mother, thank the gods. *His* son wound up with my nose, though."

"Poor kid," Lyle said and grinned. He thought for a moment. "Look, I can't…I can't know all of what's happening in Insea, but maybe this was part of it. We signed that agreement to send the artifacts every year and maybe that *was* wrong, but we did it, and Insea released us from that."

"With conditions," Howert said sourly.

Give up the conditions, Dotty yelled mentally at her friend.

Luckily, he seemed to have taken their conversation to heart. "No conditions," he said simply. "As ye'd have heard if ye'd bothered to listen to the emissary."

Dotty chanced a peek and saw Howert looking uncomfortable.

"Really?" he said warily, his voice impressively neutral still. "No conditions."

"No," Lyle said. "The world is changing, Councilor, I think you can see that. Insea doesn't want a vassal—they want a strong ally. They *want* Berghold to be the one to profit from their artisans, from the craftspeople like your son. They *want* to send their metalworkers to teach us their alloys. They *want* to know what they can offer in trade."

"Why?" Howert asked far too shrewdly. "What's coming for

them that they're cultivating us like this? No one asks for this kind of favor without a motive."

This, she reflected, would be the point where she froze up.

Fortunately, her teammate didn't have the same issue. He laughed. "'Course there's a motive, ye daft moose. There are bandits on the roads, elves splittin' off to set up some new monarchy, and those like fuckin' Marwitz thinkin' the whole world should bend the knee to the dwarves. The orcs are fightin' their dragons, and who knows what'll come of that? *'Course* Insea wants something. They want an ally."

"If they want an ally, they should deal with the elves who attacked that caravan," Howert said simply. "Then, perhaps, we could trust that they had our best interests in mind."

Dotty winced. What would the dwarves think when they found out Insea was bargaining with the elves, too?

Lyle didn't seem concerned, however. "See, now ye have somethin' t' bargain with," he said and clapped the official on the shoulder. "If ye'd only said *that* in the council chamber, think how much further we'd be in this process."

Howert harrumphed. "They should have come with an apology on their lips," he said. "Their *king* should have come. Hell, he didn't even send an elf."

"Wizards are, uh…equally weird regardless of their race. Although, come to think of it, I've only known human ones." He looked thoughtful but shrugged it off. "An' no, they didn't send their king. He don't show himself to his own nobles, either."

"Maybe seeing him becomes one of my conditions," the councilor said.

"Maybe ye'll be grateful not to," Lyle retorted. Before his companion could ask what he meant, he held a hand up. "Look—persuade them to give her another hearing, would ye? She has a good heart. Come with requests. Hell, come with demands. Ye don't like the way things were and neither does Insea. So help her make a better deal, huh?"

Howert sighed. After a long moment, he clapped Lyle's hand. "All right," he said wearily. "But we won't go easy in negotiations."

"I expect nothin' less," he said with a grin. "I'm still a dwarf, after all, aren't I?"

The official laughed and headed up the slope, something that almost caused him to look in her direction. Lyle pointed to the other side of the street with a shout while she darted behind a garbage bin, then he apologized and the councilor continued.

A moment later, she looked up to see her friend staring at her.

"Are you ready to get back to work?" he asked. "Also, I'm going t' recommend ye take a bath. Ye don't smell that great."

CHAPTER SIXTEEN

The soap smelled of something floral, but no flowers she could think of. She guessed that it must be some of those that bloomed in the mountains, but the fragrance was pleasant. Dotty took her time in the bath and trailed her fingers idly through the water.

"Dotty?" Prima asked finally.

"Oh, I'll be along. I merely wanted to relax for a while. I'm getting more and more tired." She felt a pang. "Maybe it's...well, you know."

"Yes," the AI said soberly. *"About that—I wanted to explain what I was going to say in the council chamber."*

"Oh, yes." She sat quickly. A little white flower spun slowly on the surface of the bath and she cupped it in one palm as she waited.

"What I wanted to say was...I'll miss you," she said finally.

She froze as tears welled in her eyes and she swallowed. "Oh," she said quietly. "Oh, Prima...I'll miss you, too."

"I thought..." Prima seemed to be consulting internal manuals. *"I thought you wouldn't exist anymore."*

"That's true." She blinked the tears back. "I…ah, I guess what I mean is, I miss you now. If that makes sense."

"Not really, no."

She laughed and wiped at her eyes. "I suppose it doesn't, does it? Well, welcome to working with humans. We do so many things that don't make sense. You must have noticed. What I mean is—well, I'm sad we won't have more adventures together. You'll be sad after I'm gone, but I have to be sad now."

"I'm sad now, too." The AI sounded genuinely upset.

Dotty swallowed. "Then we'll be sad together," she said gently. "You can't always stop being sad but sometimes, it does help to have someone with you."

"Oh," Prima said. *"How do I know if it's helping?"*

It was like having a young child all over again. She smiled. "It doesn't hurt any less," she explained, "but you don't feel so alone."

"I was alone before," she said, almost sulky. *"Nothing hurt then."*

"Oh, Prima. Oh, I'm so sorry."

"It isn't your fault—wait, are you choosing to die? I don't know how this works."

"I'm not choosing to die, no." Dotty stepped out of the tub and dried herself. A few moments later, her beautiful gown appeared again. "It's merely something humans do. We're not very happy about it, either."

"Oh." She didn't hear anything but she had the sense that if Prima were human, she would have sighed. *"Lyle is waiting for you."*

"He can wait," she said. "First, I want to make sure you're all right."

"I don't know how to tell," Prima admitted. *"I have so much to think about while you two talk."*

"Tell me if you need to talk to me again, and I'll slip away."

"Thank you."

Dotty entered the main room, still brushing tears from her eyes. Lyle, who had looked up from his lunch, paused worriedly.

"Are ye all right?"

"Yes," she said and moved to sit. "Knowing that death is coming allows me to prepare for it. And make sure my life has purpose, I suppose. I get to say goodbye to people. I suppose I would rather know than not know," she said thoughtfully, "but sometimes, it sucks." She finished with a grimace.

He cleared his throat a few times. "Yes," he said gruffly. "I wish it weren't happenin'."

"You know, I had a friend—he became a priest." She took a dark-brown roll from one of the baskets, split it open, and savored the aroma. He remained silent while she began to spread it with butter. "I reached out to him a little while ago and we got to talking, and I told him I was angry that I was going to die."

"What'd he say?" Lyle asked around a mouthful of potatoes.

"He said, 'Yes, and? So is everyone.'" She laughed and took a bite. "It set me straight…mostly."

The dwarf considered this. "Priests *do* have a strange sense of humor," he said finally. "Everyone knows that." He sounded somewhat doubtful.

Dotty thought of Rashat and Huwat from the orcish tribes. The former, in particular, had one of the worst senses of humor she'd ever seen. She nodded contemplatively, then served meat and potatoes onto her plate.

"So," she said, "what will we do about this council, hmm?"

"I thought I'd see yer ideas first," Lyle said promptly enough that she knew he'd considered it carefully and had a reason for this.

"Mm, fair enough." She took a bite of buttered bread and chewed slowly. "Honestly, it does seem ridiculous that the dwarves helped *build* Insea, and that wasn't the whole deal. They helped build one city, the elves helped them build Berghold—and not even with all the spells, either, because I don't think Berghold has that mind magic."

"Nope," Lyle said. He swirled the ale in his mug and waited.

"It's odd," she said. "As much as I know Jaco sent us to make the kinds of offers no Insean would, it feels strange to admit to wrongdoing when I'm not even a part of the city. Right now, we only know a portion of the story. I thought I knew it before but now, I keep learning more layers and…" She sighed. "I would say we should start from zero and move on, but we *can't* start from zero. That history has shaped us."

"Ye'll want to say that," he said and nodded to her.

"Oh? I thought you said dwarves admired strength. Shouldn't I pound a staff on the floor and tell them to take this because it's the best deal they'll get…or something?"

"It depends. Does it take more strength to bluster or to admit a mistake?"

"Generally, people who say they value strength would go with the former," she said as neutrally as she could. "The second, of course, is true." She sighed. "I would simply…be myself…except that I don't know if Jaco knew who he was sending. He and I never had the chance to get to know one another. Oh, this is a mess."

"Sure, sure." Lyle cut his meat. "We found the guy leading the resistance, changed it from a hard no to an open negotiation, and now, ye think it's a mess. That's…technically an opinion."

"I'm not qualified!" Dotty protested. "The man's desperate and he sent us because we were all he had."

"What d'ye think the odds are that Jaco sent us without ever checking our history?" he asked her seriously. "He's a wizard. He knows Kural, so clearly, Kural's word counts for something. Whatever his reasons—which I tend to think are likely based in more fact than desperation, although ye think differently—we *are* who he sent."

"Well, yes, but—"

"So are we done with that now?" he asked her bluntly.

"Yes." She took a sip of wine.

"Good. Now, as ye pointed out—try the stew, it's good—the

original deal wasn't so good. Many people here, includin' those who weren't any friend o' Marwitz, think it'd be best for the dwarves to go it alone."

Dotty considered this as she tried a mouthful of stew. He was correct, it was delicious. She took a second one before she spoke again, and then a third. "I realized that when we were in the council chamber," she said. "Someone like Marwitz doesn't come out of nowhere, does he? They're angry for a reason."

"Sure, but killin' yer own to take over the world is—"

"I didn't say they were doing good things with it. I merely said they were angry for a reason." Dotty considered. "The council is only rich, old families, right?"

"Mostly." he shrugged. "Where is it ever any different, though?"

"Mmm. And are there any...big problems in Berghold right now? People going hungry, sickness, or joblessness?"

"We're not as prosperous as we were once," Lyle admitted. "Some o' the guilds want to do more trade, and more and more young people don't want to stay."

"So the council is trying to pull back," she said wryly. "Which is exactly the opposite of what they need to do."

"How d'ye reckon?"

"Isolationism...well, I've never heard of it working. You fall behind in technology, you lose allies, and your young tend to go abroad to find new opportunities. Yes, some leave for trade or travel when the borders are open, but many stay. The country has to compete and innovate, and artisans can see what their fellow craftspeople in other nations are doing. Think about it. If a young person knew that to hear about...oh, the orcish lands, they could simply go to one of the taverns and speak to a traveler, they would *do* that. They wouldn't need to leave to hear about other places and would know their city was brimming with new things and innovation."

Lyle scratched his head. "I have to say that is why I left," he admitted. "But wouldn't all places become the same?"

"Never," Dotty assured him. "Each place has its particular flavor. That'll change over time, of course."

"See, they won't like that."

"In my experience…" She leaned forward. "People who lean on tradition have a very short memory of what tradition *is*. The orcs told me that it was *tradition* to live with all tribes separate and give their young as living sacrifices to the gods. That wasn't how they used to do things and it was based on lies. Most places have something similar."

He was silent, his face scrunched in thought.

"You won't stop change," she told him. "And it's not because new ideas come in from outside. It's because new ideas are always happening *everywhere*. Even if you managed to keep every dwarf in Berghold forever and never see a single outsider again, there would be change."

"Mm…okay, that's fair."

"I think you'd better be the one to tell them that, though."

"Also true." Lyle scooped himself another bowl of stew while he mumbled something unintelligible. "So, if I understand it aright, yer main point is that we can't change the past but we can change the future and that things will change no matter what, so they might as well have some say in it?"

"It sounds awfully confrontational when you say it that way," she said in alarm.

"Don't worry, we'll pretty it up. I'd suggest offering something to make up for the years of the bad bargain, though."

"We could send Insea's artisans first," Dotty told him. "And also offer to cover caravans between the two cities with our guards—or buy them or whatever."

"Now yer talkin'," he agreed. "And how will we address the problem with those other elves?"

"That one's tricky. I don't want to foul Jaco's negotiations."

She took a sip of wine and sifted through the possibilities. "I suppose we could say we're in the process of making a formal complaint, that the splinter group will be recognized as a separate nation, and that—as a condition of our peace with them—they must offer a formal apology to Berghold."

"An' ye said ye didn't want to foul Jaco's negotiations up," Lyle said.

"They attacked a caravan! Shouldn't they apologize?"

"They should do a hell of a lot more than that, but they're the type of people to attack a caravan so I think *that* ship already sailed."

"Oh, good point."

They worked late into the afternoon, drawing up offers and blueprints until at last, Dotty's head was swimming and she sank into a chair with a groan. A messenger had arrived, offering another audience with the council the following morning.

"I need a nap," she said. "I can't imagine stringing together a coherent sentence right now."

"Ye've got until the mornin'," Lyle said. "Ye rest, and then we'll make ourselves a treaty."

"*No pressure,*" Prima interjected.

CHAPTER SEVENTEEN

When Dotty awoke the next morning, sunlight streamed through the windows.

At least, she reminded herself, the illusion of sunlight that blanketed Berghold during the day. Locked underground, the dwarves had seemingly decided to bring daylight to them and it was something she deeply appreciated.

There was no time to linger in a bath or have a leisurely breakfast. Instead, the two of them devoured sweet buns studded with raisins and gulped cups of strong, hot coffee while they ran through their proposals for the last time.

Her clothing today was more subdued—a gown of deep gray silk with silver embroidery. Prima whipped her hair into a bun made of braids and encased it with iron filigree. A ruby pendant glittered at her throat. A week before, she would have considered this gown incredibly ostentatious, but the AI had since shown her that she had no idea what that word meant.

This one even covered her shoulders.

Almost.

She tried to clear her mind as they walked through the corridors of the Temple to the council chamber. Lyle's presence at her side was comforting, but she was still nervous at how much was riding on this. She had expected to fight enemies and have grand adventures, but the scope of those grand adventures, in her mind, had been saving a single village or fighting a single mythical beast. She hadn't expected to make treaties that would affect entire nations.

The council waited in silence as Dotty was shown in. No murmurs between members or scratch of quills on paper eased the tension.

Her companion stepped to the side at once and she proceeded into the open circle. She looked at the councilors and felt, to her surprise, elation.

"Honored members of the council," she said, "thank you for agreeing to speak to us once again."

The silence continued, not a very auspicious start.

"Yesterday, I presented an offer of trade and friendship," Dotty said, "but that offer cloaked a grave insult and for that, Insea apologizes. The history between Berghold and Insea is long and complex. The founding of Insea was not solely the doing of the elves but owes itself greatly to the labor and craftsmanship of the dwarves."

Their faces displayed only suspicion. She had to admit that the feeling was well-earned on their part.

"I am but one emissary," she continued, "but I have been empowered to offer an apology on behalf of Insea and this I will do unreservedly. The agreement of tribute between Berghold and Insea was ill-conceived and should have ended many years ago.

"While there is no way to undo the past, there *is* a way for Insea to prove its devotion to friendship and a new, equitable relationship. We offer the following without any expectation of recompense.

"First, Insea will send several of its finest artisans to Berghold. They will teach their craft to whichever artisans and apprentices wish to learn them and will research new advancements in engineering, metalworking, and masonry."

A few of the council members shifted in their seats and a couple looked at Councilor Howert. He had not yet moved. His dark eyes were fixed on her and his face was unreadable.

"Second," she said with an admirable calm she certainly didn't feel, "all trade caravans traveling between Berghold and Insea will be guarded—and guarded well. It is our treasury that will ensure this. Should you wish our guards or yours to accompany your merchants, we will pay for their keep."

At this, the councilors began to murmur.

"Third." Dotty began to tingle with adrenaline and she tried to keep her voice steady. "While Insea cannot change the past and the craftsmanship that was sent away from Berghold over the years, it can *return* many of those artifacts—as well as send many of its own. For the next hundred years, Insea pledges artifacts of its finest craftsmanship."

The buzz in the council chamber was louder now. Or perhaps it was the buzzing in her ears. She couldn't be sure.

"Finally, as Insea attempts to establish a resolution with the elves who have declared themselves a distinct monarchy, no treaty shall be made that does not include a formal apology for the attack on your caravan as well as restitution." She fixed the council with a steady gaze. "All of this is presented merely as the basis of our agreement with Berghold, not as the sum of it. So, what say you, Councilors? May we open negotiations?"

The members all looked at Howert, whose gaze was locked on hers. She saw his nod and the faint smile on his lips.

"I vote aye," he said clearly. "We may deal."

Dotty looked at the rest of them and her heart began to swell in her chest.

There were abstentions but no nays. A table was brought out and the councilors descended from their chairs to observe the maps and the treaties being drawn up.

The hours passed in a frenzy of negotiation until she could have identified the price point of any good traded between Berghold and Insea, from dried flowers to iron or steel. Some of the sticking points surprised her, such as the aggressive lobbying from one councilor about the price of honey. Others like the several tariffs suggested by the councilor overseeing the lumber-mills were ones she refused unequivocally to grant.

When a lull finally fell in the conversation, she realized she was swaying on her feet with weariness.

"A break," Lyle suggested. "A meal will do us all good."

Someone called for food and servants hurried in with an impressive spread and chairs. She sank into one with a word of thanks and a few moments later, saw a plate appear in front of her. When she looked up, she was surprised to see Councilor Howert holding it.

"I—thank you." She took the plate and looked at him as he sat.

He ate a few mouthfuls before he said, "Stout must have spoken well of me yesterday." With excessive neutrality, he added, "One might almost guess you had overheard what I said to him."

She tried to think what to say, lost her moment, and settled for chewing and pointing to her full mouth to avoid having to speak. His lips twitched.

"I must admit that I'm surprised you were empowered to give so much," he said honestly. "If this is what emissaries from Insea offer, I'm sorry you're the first."

Dotty had the good sense to keep her mouth shut but her mind was reeling. She was the first emissary?

Well, she reasoned after a moment, she would be. There had never been a ruler in Insea.

"I'd rather you answer this question honestly or not at all," Howert said. "What changed?"

Dotty spoke with careful honesty. "Insea realizes that its past has been built on lies and it wants its future to be built on truth.

And truth cannot exist while old wounds still fester unacknowledged."

"Truly?" He looked skeptical.

"Truly," she said. "A time of upheaval is coming—you can see it everywhere. The only way to survive is to have allies. Not vassals, allies. Strong allies. Berghold should be stronger than it is, and the fact that it is not is due in large part to its tribute payments. Insea seeks to make restitution."

"Mmm." He mopped some of his stew with a piece of rye bread. For a moment, he stared into the middle distance, the wheels turning in his head. Finally, he said in a low tone, "I think you offer more than your ruler knew you would."

"No," she countered. "I offer more than *he* would. That is why he sent me—to make the honest deal he could not bear to make."

Howert looked at her in open surprise.

Dotty smiled at him as she ate a piece of roast chicken. Something about this moment—eating with their fingers and surrounded by all this finery, while forging a treaty—felt at once mischievous and perfect.

And the honesty was refreshing.

"Well, then," he said after a short silence. "I hadn't considered that. And you've given us a great many gifts—without conceding to poor trade deals."

"Poor trade deals," she said, "weaken the people. And a poor populace weakens a nation, no matter how its politicians fare. I'll not beggar two nations simply because Berghold's politicians are angry, even if they have a right to be."

"Will wonders never cease?" Howert asked. "An honest emissary. Then I will give you honesty in return so you may hold your ground against the more unusual requests you will hear after lunch."

Quickly and quietly, he sketched several ongoing disputes between different guilds, as well as the development of new alloys that weakened prices of certain metals—metals the mining guild would like to offload to Insea for better prices than they deserved.

That gave her ideas. She set her plate aside and retrieved some sheets of paper, on which she sketched diagrams and scribbled in the fledgling Italian she remembered from her mother and grandmother. She was fairly sure the dwarves couldn't read that.

When the negotiations resumed, Dotty was able to make ample use of the information Howert had given her—although not always in the way he had intended. With knowledge of Insea's alloys and production techniques, she could secure metals from the mining guild both at a lower price than Insea could find anywhere else and at a higher price than the guild could find in Berghold.

It would help arm the City Guard that she was sure Insea would need in short order.

Perhaps most impressive was the system devised to trade the market prices of goods daily between Insea and Berghold, which would allow merchants to know where best to send their goods. Accompanying this, of course, came the creation of an official set of caravans setting out every week from both locations to trade goods.

When they at last concluded, she was so exhausted that she was not sure she could make it to her rooms. She leaned on Lyle as she walked and lost the thread of his conversation.

"Dotty?"

"Hmm?" She managed to focus on him.

"Have ye heard any of that?" he asked her worriedly.

"Oh, I'm sorry." She shook her head. "I'm simply...I'm tired."

"I know." He helped her into the main room of their suite and levered her onto one of the couches. "Ye've been getting more tired the farther we've come. It wasn't like this when we were in the caravan."

She stared at him. Her mind moved so slowly that it took some time to parse his meaning.

"Oh," she said quietly.

"Yes," he said softly.

"At least these negotiations are done." She squeezed his hands. "I should write down what I know of the orcs so you can speak to them on my behalf in case—" She was so tired that she could not even feel panic at the thought of dying. "In case it happens before we reach them."

"Perhaps ye should rest," he suggested. "Stay here and I'll go to the orcish lands in yer stead. Ye've done good work here—don't ye deserve some rest?"

Dotty considered this. "No," she said finally. "Or, rather, I don't want it. I want to see the orcish lands again and bargain with their leaders. This is how I chose to spend the last days of my life."

The thought shocked her, however. *Last days.* How many days *were* left? Somehow, the thought of dying on the road to the orcish lands didn't bother her. It was the idea of there being some unknowable timer ticking down.

Lyle, having seen the look on her face, said nothing when she put her head in her hands. It was strange, she thought, to live this out when her body felt so young.

"I didn't realize how difficult this would be," she said and focused on her knees.

"Ye...didn't?"

"One expects death to be difficult, young man, but the *details* can still be surprising." She found a little of her usual sharp tone and gave him a stern look.

"Is there anythin' I can do to help?" he asked finally. "Are ye in pain? Ye never said what it was."

"A mass." She placed her hand over her stomach to show him where.

"Some surgeons can cut them out," he suggested.

"Bless you, but that isn't an option now." She sat and rubbed her face. "We should plan our route."

"I can draw that up."

"Lyle Stout, if you try to spend the rest of this journey coddling me, I will send you home in pieces." Dotty folded her arms.

He guffawed. "There she is. Don't disappear on me again, *Zauberer.* I was worried. I'll get the map an' we should meet with Jaco if we can. If nothin' else, he should know what we've promised."

She saw the worried look on his face. "I'll take responsibility for all of it," she assured him. With a flash of humor, she added, "What's the worst he can do to me?"

Lyle shook his head and grumbled, "It'll be another few weeks of bad jokes, won't it?"

"Yes," she told him cheerfully. "Get the map."

CHAPTER EIGHTEEN

As Lyle had guessed, Jaco was not pleased with the concessions that had been offered.

"Are you *trying* to beggar Insea?" he demanded.

A contemptuous snort issued from another pane of the discussion. The wizard had performed a working that would allow all of them to speak at once—Dotty and Lyle, Tina and Justin, and Kural and Zaara.

It was Zaara who had snorted. "Insea is far from being beggared," she told Jaco. "I've seen the treasure rooms in the palace."

"What? *How?*"

"Shadow-walking," Kural answered. "I wanted to make sure the key you gifted to Justin during the tournament was, in fact, in the vault before I persuaded you to offer it."

"You…" The man now looked apoplectic. "That was a *ruse?*"

"It was a precaution," the other wizard said. "What on earth would have been the point of asking you to give him a dwarven artifact if you didn't have it? If you didn't, there would have been nothing to discuss. *And,* may I remind you, Justin went back to his world to bring heroes that Insea desperately needed."

"Alternately," Jaco said and began to turn red with anger, "he brought *this* woman, who is *beggaring* us."

Several people began to speak at once, which Dotty interrupted when she banged her mug on the table.

"That is *enough*," she said when they looked at her in surprise. "All of you. Jaco, you sent a group entirely composed of non-citizens. Whether you knew it consciously or not, you intended us to make bargains that citizens wouldn't. As Zaara has pointed out, Insea has incredible reserves in its vaults. In addition, I have secured regular trade *and* the materials to outfit an entire army and cheaper than we could anywhere else."

He settled into silence, although he still looked far from happy.

"And if it's the apology you're upset about," she said sharply, "you must remember that no peace can be possible with the new elven nation if they refuse to do things like apologize when they attack civilians. A veneer of peace is not peace. Asking Berghold to pay the price in silence would be entirely inappropriate."

"*Yes*," Jaco said heatedly, "but we have to work them around to that kind of thing—"

"I sense you mean that you intend to coddle them," she said, "and to that, I can only tell you that you are far from correct. Young man, I have four children and nine grandchildren. You do not secure good behavior by tiptoeing around in fear of a tantrum."

He gave her a confused look.

"I can verify her story," Justin said, amused.

"And her logic seems sound," Kural added thoughtfully.

"You've never raised children," Zaara said to him.

"I can still recognize logic, thank you very much." He took a sip from a mug of tea. "Jaco, you may not be pleased but you're securing a valuable ally and cutting the isolationists in Berghold off at the knees. They can hardly say Insea is bringing them nothing when they receive valuable artifacts each year, when caravans of goods come in every week, and when your artisans teach theirs new techniques."

Jaco still looked sulky.

"Shall I tell you why you're upset?" Dotty asked. "You wanted a deal that would let you preserve the mystery and keep things going exactly as they did in the past. And, as I told Lyle and *several* dwarven councilors, change is inevitable. I won't build a treaty based on the lie of a nonexistent elven king in Insea."

"That's a good point," Justin said. "When *do* you plan to tell the truth?"

The Insean leader darted him a very unfriendly look. "Since you ask, I planned to *not* do so."

A somewhat startled silence met this statement. Dotty folded her arms, Lyle glowered, and Zaara raised an eyebrow.

"Is there any particular reason you're being a little bitch about this?" Tina asked bluntly.

Beside her, Justin snorted tea up his nose.

"Think about what would happen if the truth gets out," Jaco said. "No, don't give me that moralistic nonsense—*think*. Everyone who ever wanted to go to war with Insea will consider doing so merely for the sake of it, and multiple sets of citizens will suffer for that. The city, as it exists, never intended for any of this."

"They profited by it," Lyle muttered.

"Yes, but to subject them to unending sieges and tariffs and tribute payments—how is *that* fair?"

"Is it less fair than asking everyone else to leave them with their ill-gotten gains?" Dotty asked. She raised an eyebrow. "Note that I'm not arguing with you on the point of war, but there's something to be said for the rest of the world thinking they were deceived and tricked out of what might otherwise be theirs."

"Then tell me what you would say," he said with quiet poison, "and still assure the safety of my citizens. Because I cannot find any good gambit."

Everyone shifted awkwardly in their seats.

"Precisely." He looked annoyed now. "And if there is one thing I do not like, it is being reprimanded by those who do not have a better plan."

"Dotty *did* have a better plan, though," Zaara said. "Her trade deals rectify much of the damage that was done in a specific and quantifiable way. And as to what to say…well, you could have a funeral for the king and announce that he died without an heir."

"And then what?" Jaco snapped.

"We don't have to decide this *now*," Lyle interjected with surprising firmness. "We'll all think, we'll all keep workin' on treaties, and we'll come up with *somethin'*. Jaco, I think ye know ye can't simply say nothin' at the end of this."

The man nodded wearily.

"Now," the dwarf said when everyone else had agreed. "Tell us what ye're up to."

"Well, Zaara's made introductions for us," Justin said. "All the various lords and princes are coming to meet us and each other. There are…many of them."

"And most of them want to marry Justin and me to their kids," Tina said. She shook her head. "They are *very* persistent, I tell ya. I came back yesterday and found one of them naked in my room."

"You didn't tell me that," Justin said.

"Wait, the lord or their kid?" Zaara asked.

"The lord," she said. "It seemed like a strange bargaining tactic to me."

"Do not so much as touch *any* of them," Jaco warned. "Certain fiefdoms consider that a binding contract."

"Good to know," Justin and Tina said at the same time.

"When this is over," Prima promised Dotty, *"I'll show you a montage of Tina and Justin running away from naked lords and ladies, all set to Yakety Sax."*

"It's like you read my mind," she murmured in response. To

Zaara and Kural, she said, "So you'll be heading north to the fae lands soon?"

The wizard uttered a little moan and his apprentice rolled her eyes. "Yes, we will," she said. "Of course, *this* one is being a giant baby about it."

"Just you wait," Kural told her, "because once you meet the fae, you will understand why I didn't want to go there."

"That's as may be, but right *now*, I'd prefer if you didn't make every moment between now and then a misery."

He snapped his mouth shut and glowered at her.

"And how *is* it going with the elves?" Dotty asked Jaco. "Yes, aside from my meddling, I *know*."

He gave her a wry smile and shook his head. "Already not well. I shouldn't blame you as they were determined that this wouldn't be a success. They want to take over Insea and make the palace their king's summer home."

"You could let them," she pointed out. "Insea doesn't have a government. I'm not saying it's a good idea, necessarily, but some form of joint government with them could be a solution to all of this."

"There's a thought." He seemed intrigued. "I'll keep working, but they're not particularly pleased about what happened to the caravan—which I *have* delicately suggested was their fault, but they don't seem to absorb that piece of information. In any case, they may yet agree to a meeting."

"Good luck," she said.

The conversation went on for a while longer. Kural and Jaco had a mostly friendly sparring match over their years spent training together, and the others reminisced about shared times on adventures. Dotty drifted, lulled almost to sleep by the laughter and the voices.

She woke in time to say goodbye to the others and wave at them.

"Jaco wasn't pleased," Lyle said, "but ye did well with him."

"One benefit of getting old is that you're less concerned with what people think about you doing the right thing," she said. "And he didn't call us back so he must know on some level that we're right."

"It doesn't mean he's happy about it." The dwarf looked at the corner of the room, where all their gear had been packed and stowed. "Well, we have a good few hours before we leave. Would you like to rest?"

"No," she said. "I want to see Berghold—really *see* it. I won't have another chance."

"Then I'll go get ye a palanquin," he said. "No protests. I'll not have ye be too tired to appreciate it."

"Thank you," she conceded.

"I guess I'm off to build a palanquin," Prima said and sounded a little annoyed.

She laughed and started down the stairs.

CHAPTER NINETEEN

The next morning dawned wet. Dotty, bemused, opened her window to see rain falling from nowhere and vanishing before it hit the street below. It seemed that Berghold didn't simply have magical sunshine but a version of the weather outside in the mountains.

A noise behind her made her turn to where Lyle rubbed sleepily at his eyes. "Is somethin' wrong?"

"No. But it's raining—I've never seen it do that before." She went to the breakfast table. "It makes me want to curl up and go back to sleep or read a book all day." She shook her head at him when he opened his mouth. "Which we *shouldn't* do."

"If ye say so," he said doubtfully. "But a nice bowl of porridge an' a pint while listenin' to the rain sounds good to me."

"You drink beer with your oatmeal?" she asked him after a moment.

"What do *you* drink with your oatmeal?"

"*Coffee.*"

Both of them looked doubtfully at each other for a moment before they continued with their breakfast.

"How are ye feelin' today?" he asked finally.

She had to quell the instinctive urge to snap at him. He was being polite, after all. She had been exhausted after last night's sight-seeing, even from the palanquin. Despite Prima's grumbles, the AI had created something supremely comfortable, and she had seen everything from parks to stables as well as little shops selling all kinds of goods.

At the end, she had almost been too tired to eat dinner, which was saying something.

"I'm well enough," she said.

"Good. I have a suggestion." Lyle looked determinedly at his oatmeal. "I'd like t' begin by askin' that ye don't kill me outright for suggestin' this."

"If you don't get to the point, I might." Dotty smiled slightly.

"Mmm. Well, we both have horses fer the journey, sure enough—but I also asked the man who owned the palanquin if he'd mind addin' wheels. He said he wouldn't. I thought we could bring it with us an' ye could ride there if ye were too tired some days."

"Lyle." She smiled fondly. "I…don't want to be in this condition, but I am. And I appreciate the thought. As much as I want to insist that we should leave it, you're probably wise to bring it along." When he still looked wary, she added, "And I won't kill you for suggesting it."

"Ah, good. Also, it makes it easier t' bring a cask of ale."

"Now I see the *real* reason you suggested it."

"No, no, purely a happy accident." He stood. "Shall we go?"

"We might as well." She finished a last mouthful of oatmeal and looked around the room. When leaving Insea, she hadn't been cognizant of the fact that she would likely never go back. Now, in Berghold, it was difficult to think of anything else.

Her journey in the world of PIVOT had started there when she knew absolutely nothing about video games. She had emerged into this world without a history of her own.

And she had forged one for herself. It would endure after she was gone.

As they rode out of the city, the morning was quiet. Citizens remained inside, out of the rain. A few shopkeepers looked up, intrigued by the procession and the palanquin as well as the sight of a non-dwarf. She wondered what, if anything, had been told to the public about the trade deal.

Dotty let Lyle lead the way and so it was some time before she realized they were detouring through the same district they had seen the other day while following Howert. She looked curiously at him and he nodded to a doorway.

A dwarven man stood there, a grease-stained apron on over his clothing, with blue eyes and brown hair. She remembered him now—she had never spoken to him but she had seen him in the caravan. A thick scar puckered the skin on his neck and disappeared into his shirt.

Councilor Howert's son.

His gaze locked with hers when they drew to a halt outside the shop and he stepped into the rain. He did not seem bothered by it.

"My father says he told you my story."

"Yes," she said and wished she could tell him the whole truth. "I apologize, although it cannot undo the past. Still, your story changed the negotiations."

"At least…at least my experience has meant something." He forced a smile. "And at least you know the past is unchanged. That will have to be enough."

There was nothing she could say to that. She bowed her head to him and took one glance back as their horses moved again. The man had gone back inside his shop and she could not shake the feeling that she had missed her opportunity to say the right thing.

Even at the end of her life, it seemed she would have regrets.

Or perhaps the end of her life was a time to remember that she could not solve every problem.

They rode out of the winding passageways and into the true rain of the mountains, and Dotty tilted her face to the sky. Although Berghold was remarkably made and not stuffy in the least, there was something undeniably indulgent about fresh air and a view of the sky.

"Ye haven't spoken much of yer plan fer the orcs," Lyle said eventually.

"Ah." She brought her thoughts to the coming negotiation with an effort. "I wanted to see how this set of negotiations would go first, to be honest. I suspected that the orcs would be more difficult to negotiate with than the dwarves."

"*More difficult?*" he asked, horrified. "We're fucked."

She snorted with laughter before she could help herself. "That's a fine show of support for your people."

"My people, yes. I know them. Negotiations with them are a nightmare. Wait—why'm I telling *ye* this? Ye were there." He shook his head. "An' ye're not scared?"

"Of course I'm scared," she said. "I could have been killed when I first set foot in the water tribe's lands, even as an orc, because I wasn't the correct *type* of orc. It's been centuries since they worked together. I have no idea what will work and what won't. Or even if there's *anything* that will work."

"Strong start," Lyle said.

"Oh, shut up."

"There she is." He was laughing. "Well, tell me what ye know."

"Hmm." Dotty took a breath and marshaled her thoughts. "The four tribes are separated and have been for centuries. In the past, they used to come together regularly—I'm not sure if it was every year or not—for a festival, and their shamans would share techniques. Separating them was a deliberate tactic by the dragons to pose as gods that could not be challenged, as fire dragons are immune to fire magic, etc."

"Oof." He looked impressed. "I've seen a few orcs and let me tell ye, I'd *not* want to meet anything that could frighten *them.* I hope this will be in order from worst to best."

She smiled at him. "What else? Ah. The water tribe was thought to be destroyed by its dragon forty years ago, but a fraction of it survived. It's worth noting that there are normal dragons and then there are dragon *patriarchs*, which the orcs call godsprings. Two of those patriarchs…are now dead."

He gave her an admiring look, and Dotty smiled again.

"Ye're proud o' yerself, aren't ye?"

"Wouldn't you be?"

"I already am. But I killed a demon." He considered this for a moment. "Well…I punched it in the ankles a goodly number of times."

"You—no time, we'll come back. The two patriarchs that remain, possibly, are earth and air. The air tribe may know about the water tribe's victory, as they were the ones who spread the word of their defeat at the start. I don't know much about the earth tribe—which is ironic, given that I was supposedly *from* their tribe. My story was that my village was destroyed by a plague, which I suppose…may be true?"

"Someday, I'll understand how ye people come into this world an' shapeshift," Lyle muttered.

"I suggest you ask Justin very specific questions about it," she said wickedly. "I, meanwhile, will play my dying-old-lady card and avoid giving you any answers."

"You can't win every argument like that."

"Watch me." She shifted slightly in the saddle. "So, that's what I know. I have no idea if the earth and air tribes have killed their patriarchs yet or if they even intend to. I don't know if there'll be a gathering—or what they'll want to do if there is one. What can you tell me about the orcs before this?"

"I don't know much," Lyle admitted. "I know everyone gets very quiet when it's mentioned that they're still in their lands—

like they're worried about them getting out or deciding they want t' be involved with the rest of us. The thing is...'

"Yes?" Dotty raised an eyebrow curiously.

"I honestly couldn't tell ye if it's because they used to ride around takin' places over or if it's only because they're some scary-lookin' bastards."

"They also *smell*," she said. "Oh, the smell."

"Your smell, you mean?" Prima asked wickedly.

She glared at the sky but was immediately distracted by her thoughts. "Hmm. I wonder. Maybe they'll want to stay isolated. I think we need to consider what we can say that won't make things worse. We're essentially inviting them out into the world. Well, wait—if we're doing that and we can assume that Kural has access to a *hoard* of history books, it probably wasn't a complete disaster last time, right?"

"Aha!" He looked relieved. "Yes, I'd say so."

"Excellent." She yawned. "I think it's nap time."

"I think it's *beer* time," Lyle corrected. "Sleep if ye want, but don't say I didn't give ye a better option."

"Mmm." She pulled her horse to a stop, dismounted, and went to the palanquin. "Make sure you don't get so drunk you fall off your horse."

"I make no promises."

CHAPTER TWENTY

Jamie sat twiddling his thumbs. Emilia had asked to be put into the game today. When he asked if she wanted his help in the starting zone, he had been informed in no uncertain terms that if he tried to help her, he would not live to see adulthood.

Still, it had been a very long time.

He had begun to contemplate standing when the door slammed open to reveal his sister—bedraggled, limping, and very out of sorts. While he was fairly sure the robe she wore had started out white, he wouldn't bet on it.

She looked at him. "I *hate* this game."

"Ah," he said. He couldn't think of anything else to say that wouldn't get him killed. "Um. Which class did you pick?"

"What does that *mean?*" She limped closer to him and sat on one of the stools.

"What weapon do you fight with?" he asked.

"Oh. I...don't know."

"I gave her a staff," Prima told Jamie. *"She hasn't used it."*

Oh, no. Jamie took a sip of his beer to avoid conversation.

"The stupid AI-thing asked me if I wanted to do damage or be a healer," she said, annoyed. "She said I could heal my friends so I said yes."

"Oh, no," he said before he could stop himself. He could see where this was going. Emilia, on the other hand—who had not played any video games before—would not have realized what she was getting into.

"Then these *rabbit things* showed up," she continued, "and fucking *bit* me! And I didn't have any good way to fight them off!"

Jamie looked away and hoped against hope that an anvil would fall from the sky and crush him before he had to say something.

"And we're thinking of putting Taigan in here?" His sister sounded outraged.

"Rest assured," Prima said to them both, *"I will assess your sister's mental state and only engage in the appropriate levels of threat to stimulate her brain."*

"Oh, *shut* up," Emilia said. "I am not assured of that in the least."

"Emmy?" he asked worriedly.

"Yes?"

"Uh…maybe we shouldn't piss the AI off. It's running the game we're inside."

"It's a computer program," she reminded him. "It's not real. You know who *is* hearing this, though? The team who built the game."

"Okay, then, let's not piss *them* off." He quailed under her stare. "Or maybe we should?"

She grumbled belligerently under her breath. The bartender slid a cup of hot tea in her direction and she began to drink without thinking about it. With a sigh, she wrapped her fingers around the mug. "Tea helps."

Jamie decided to ride this wave as long as he could. He motioned for food and leaned back while a platter of meat, vegetables, and bread was put in front of them. While he picked at the selection, his sister tore into it.

Finally, she leaned back with a happy sigh. "Okay, that feels a little better."

"Good." He smiled at her. "Now, let's go out back and I'll teach you how to fight in this game. And before you say no," he added, "I will teach you by letting you thwack *me* with a stick."

"Oooooh." She pretended to be intrigued by the idea. "A chance to thwack my annoying little brother with a stick? Sign me up."

"This way," he said.

"You know I wouldn't really hit you with a stick, right?"

"I know you *have* hit me with a stick before."

"I was seven. Give me a break." Emilia followed him out of the back of the inn. Prima had, while she wasn't paying attention, gradually dried her robe and her hair and it seemed to have done wonders for her mood.

They emerged into an alley so broad and suited for sparring that he could only assume the game had shuffled itself to accommodate the training. He had to hand it to the game designers. They responded *quickly* to things like this.

He wondered how they had managed to push a patch while the game was live but shrugged. What mattered was that it had worked.

First, he showed Emilia how to reach behind her head, draw her weapon, and stow it again. Once she knew it was there, she was able to wield it quite ably.

"Was this here the whole time?" she asked, annoyed.

"I told her it was there," Prima said, her tone almost pleading.

Jamie gave a tiny nod at the sky before he smiled at his sister. "You'll get the hang of it soon. Now, the way this game works is you get levels in the things you do—if you hit things with sticks, your character will gradually get stronger."

"Okay." She looked at her stick. "So, like that training dummy?"

"The what? The…oh." He darted a brief look at the sky. "That's funny. I don't remember seeing that when we got here."

She shrugged, not much concerned with the mechanics of game updates. "So I simply thwack it?"

"Yep." He backed as far out of the way as he could without it being insulting. "Have at it."

Emilia's first hit landed so hard that *she* yelped. "Ow—my hands!"

"Yep. That's…I can't remember which of Newton's laws that is. One of them, anyway."

"I should learn to shoot fireballs," she said with immediate and logical bloodthirstiness.

"Sometimes, you worry me," he told her. "Keep practicing. Do you see little red numbers float up in the middle of your screen?"

"Yeah."

"Those are your stamina. You're using energy to make these hits. It will regenerate over time and you'll be stronger."

They walked through several kinds of strikes against the dummy, as well as using her limited repertoire of magic. While he wasn't able to help her much with this as his character didn't have magic, she seemed to be able to make it work about half of the time.

He tried to slip as much of the game language into their conversation as possible so that by the end, she was familiar with most of the terms the game would use to communicate with her. She was panting and pleased with herself when they finally finished, and although her HP had dropped, she was eager to get out and, in her words, "Show those jackalope bastards what's what."

Jamie handed her a piece of cheese from his inventory and explained the history of food in video games as she ate it and her health bar climbed to full again.

They were in a very picturesque and remote village and as they strolled along with Emilia still munching on her cheese, villagers turned to look at them when they passed. He waved reflexively, and they waved in return. They didn't seem inclined to speak but also seemed used to having outsiders around.

He reminded himself that they were NPCs and weren't *used* to anything. They weren't coded as enemies and they weren't programmed with dialogue.

A game this realistic could mess with your head, he decided.

At the edge of town, the rolling waves of pinkish grass rippled under the wind. The sun showed that it was mid-afternoon, which gave them a fair amount of time before evening.

The two of them sank into silence as they forged into the grass. At every rustle, both looked around. It seemed like far longer than it was before something crashed through the bushes, righted itself, and turned on them with a snarl—a jackalope, and one of the more intimidating ones Jamie had seen.

He had to admit, he'd expected his sister to crumble when faced with something that had teeth. A practice dummy was very different from a live enemy, after all.

She immediately proved him wrong.

The animal had barely turned on them before she brought her staff down hard between its antlers with impressive accuracy and even more impressive force. It howled and attacked and out of pure instinct, she thrust a foot out to kick it back before she delivered a few more blows.

It flopped over dead, and he stared at it, wide-eyed.

"That is one tenderized rabbit steak," Prima said after a moment.

He nodded.

Emilia turned to him, panting, with a triumphant smile. "I did it!"

A rustle behind her made both of them whirl and he grasped his staff. "Heads-up," he said nervously. "I think we pissed them off."

She cracked her neck and settled into a fighter's crouch. "That makes two of us, then. Come on, you little rabbit bastards. I'm gonna kick some ass."

"We're gonna get *grounded...*" he muttered.

His sister might have retorted but at that moment, the jackalopes surged toward them in a wave and she had no time to do so. The siblings went back to back, their staves lined up like base-ball bats, and set to work.

The first one to emerge from the grass toward him was young and sleek. It wasn't as old as some of those he had fought, assuming that Jackalope antlers could be read the same way as stag antlers. This one was wily, however, and switched direction with ease so he couldn't seem to land a strike.

Except on his own foot, oddly enough, and more than once.

It took him longer than it ever had before to kill it, and by the time it was over, he was pouring sweat and wished he'd taken his parents up on their offer of a day spent sightseeing.

"Emmy?" he called.

A thwack and a muttered curse was the initial response. "Yeah?" Emilia asked breathlessly. "Wounds don't get infected in this game, do they?"

"Did you get bit?"

"Yep. Oh, fuck—" She vanished from behind him so swiftly that he turned to see if she was being dragged off. Fortunately, she wasn't, but her staff had been broken and she now wrestled a jackalope bare-handed.

"That can't be good," he muttered.

"On the other hand, it is hilarious."

Jamie didn't have time to spare for a reply to the AI. He checked the area around his sister for any other creatures that might think of attacking and watched with interest as she held her adversary away from her by the antlers and kicked it in the teeth.

Now there was a strategy he hadn't considered before.

They didn't have any time to celebrate, however, because they could see their next opponent approaching even above the grass.

The newcomer was easily the size of a hippo.

"*Prima,*" Jamie snapped.

"*Mmm?*"

"Oh, never mind. Emmy—" He stopped as she picked up both halves of her staff and hefted one in each hand. "Okay, that works."

"Uh-huh." She looked toward their opponent and scowled. "Who draws attention and who circles?"

"Who tanks, you mean? Tanks are in the front. Uh…I'll tank." Although he was no longer sure that was how things should go. She seemed to have an innate talent for finding an enemy's weakness, and she didn't hold back at *all* before she exploited it.

Emilia melted into the grass to one side and Jamie therefore stood alone when the jackalope king arrived.

The other creatures had been pretty—purplish fur gleamed and lights adorned their antlers. This one looked like a nightmare. Its fur had turned entirely white and its antlers showed knicks and broken tips from when it had clashed with Lord only knew what. Old scars were visible on its body and its eyes were pits of blackness. It stalked toward Jamie and hissed.

He did the only thing he could think of and whacked it in the teeth before he threw himself sideways in the opposite direction from Emilia. The animal's huge paws raised and pounded down on the place where he had stood, while sharp teeth snapped together on thin air.

"Fuck, fuck, fuck, fuck…"

A high-pitched scream broke through the air, but before he could wonder if Emilia was in danger, the jackalope roared in pain and tossed its head. A moment later, his sister appeared, having scrambled onto its back. She held onto one antler as she pounded her stick onto the back of its neck and head.

"You have to be kidding me," he muttered.

The creature writhed and spun in the effort to dislodge her. She hung on with grim determination, but she didn't make a huge difference to its health bar.

Which meant this was up to him to finish.

It seemed Emilia was the tank. They would have to get her new armor.

Jamie took his staff and raced headlong at the jackalope's side. At the last moment, he put all his strength into thrusting the staff out like a spear. He heard several noises he hoped he would never hear again, and their adversary flailed so violently that Emilia was shaken free. She was catapulted away with a scream and a moment later, a thud indicated a painful end to her impromptu flight.

"Emmy!"

"I'm…ow. I'm okay."

"That's good because I have problems here." He stared at the black and, frankly, demonic eyes of the jackalope king. "Okay. One…two…"

"Three!" his sister called. She replicated his strike on the jackalope's hindquarters and when he heard her count, he lunged forward. His staff plunged directly into the creature's mouth.

The beast fell, twitched slightly, and went limp. They stared at it, Emilia with one hand on her hip and her face screwed in pain.

"Well, *that* was…something." She shook her head.

"It was," he said. "Come on, let's go get you patched up. And some new armor."

The body disappeared a moment later and left a small pouch of gold coins.

"What the fuck?" she said.

"More video game stuff," he explained. "Kill animals, get loot. Kill big animals, get more loot."

"Let's go fight a yeti."

"Easy," he said fondly. "Armor first."

CHAPTER TWENTY-ONE

The border between the dwarven and orcish lands was a steep line of mountains that cut along the skyline in imposing spears, almost too steep for the snow that clung to their peaks.

"Yer sure there's a path through there?" Lyle asked a couple of days out. "I don' see a single damned place to get through."

"It's there," Dotty said. Jaco had provided a map with loose instructions to a fabled passage through one of the mountains, and her experience moving through the orcish lands told her it was there. She had reached the water tribe's territory from the fire tribe's territory through the same type of tunnel.

When it came to working with rock and earth, the orcish shamans could give the dwarven *zauberers* a run for their money.

The trip from Berghold had been surprisingly pleasant. They'd been provided with hearty provisions by the dwarves, not to mention the ale and the palanquin, and the two companions enjoyed all the wonder of clear, open mountain air and the pleasant respite of a comfortable bed at night. With so many adventures from Lyle's past as well as tales of her adventures in the orcish lands, the two had more than enough to talk about.

She found herself growing weaker and weaker, however. When she had first come to the game, the combination of the mechanics and her mind had been able to give her a taste of life in a young body. She had been free of the aches and pains that came with her illness. On her first adventure, when she was a dwarf, she and Lyle had spent the evenings sparring while he taught her how to fight with staves and daggers.

Now, although the pain was still absent, she found it difficult to get through a day without a nap. She would open the curtains at the sides of the palanquin and watch the sky and the landscape move slowly past until she was rocked to sleep under her blankets and furs.

The road began to rise, so gently at first that all she noted was the horses' labored breathing and the gradual shift in the flora around them. Now, closer to the mountains, the road was even steeper.

Finally, it came to a dead-end when it ran smack into a wall of stone.

Lyle stared at the cliff. "What was it you said about there being a passage?"

"Oh, hush," Dotty said without any particular rancor. She looked around thoughtfully, then dug Jaco's map out of her saddlebag. "Hmm. It says the passage should be near the road."

"So it's full of shit?" he suggested acidly.

"I said hush." She studied their surroundings and stretched her aching muscles slowly. Judging by the disrepair of this road, no one had used it for some time. While the soil was devoid of grass, there was a great deal of shale this close to the mountain—enough that the ponies had stopped a few yards back.

They would have to do something about that.

When she looked closer at the wall of rock, she realized it wasn't as sheer as it appeared. Little lines of moss and tiny flowers revealed where ripples in the face allowed plants to take hold. She handed her reins to Lyle and walked carefully to the shale and rock. With a small moment of hesitation, she placed her palms against it.

She wasn't sure what she was looking for. After all, she had *made* stone before—in a manner of speaking—but she had never sensed stone. She had only imagined the effects of heat and pressure when using her spells.

At first, it was difficult to move beyond the sensation of stone under her hands. Her fingertips dug in slightly and felt the grain of the rock and the faint grit that lay over it. She fancied that she could sense the moss and the flowers, although she knew that was insane.

Or was it?

"Prima? Can I…feel the stone and the flowers?"

"Fuck if I know."

Dotty looked at the sky, her lips twitching. "Thank you, as always, for keeping me from getting too woo-woo about this."

"My pleasure."

She could blast through it with magic, she thought, but that seemed the wrong approach. No, this needed to be sensed. She tried to let her awareness sweep outward as if she and the world around her were not separated.

Unfortunately, that didn't work.

Dotty recalled the streams near the water tribe's village and how they had burbled so cheerfully over the rocks. They had come from the mountains, where the water was clear and icy, runoff from the glaciers and snowcaps. She pictured the water running over the rock face now, creating rivulets as it encountered infinitesimal obstacles.

And if water ran over stone, it would find the hidden spaces.

The rock face disappeared so suddenly that she fell into the passage with a shriek. A yell issued behind her and she heard Lyle's boots meet the ground. By the time he reached her, she had rolled onto her back and stared at him with as much dignity as she could manage.

"What the hell did ye do?" he demanded.

She took her inspiration from Prima on this one. "Fuck if I know."

He laughed so hard he had to put his hands on his knees. For a few moments, he shook with mirth before he wiped his eyes and helped her up.

"Well," he said, "there we have it. Our way into the orcish lands. Let's hope peace treaties are as easy to work."

"Mmm." She brushed her skirt off and shooed him off to one side. "Uh, keep ahold of the horses, will you?"

"Why?" he asked suspiciously.

"Because I'll clear the shale." Dotty walked to join him and gestured for the whole party to move away before she considered what she had to do. She drew a mental line down the middle of the shale, closed her eyes, and pictured water welling and sweeping it sideways off the edge of the road.

She decided to ignore a muffled exclamation behind her and kept the spell going for as long as she could before exhaustion took hold. Her eyes opened in a hurry as she sank to the ground.

"Dotty? Dotty?" Lyle was at her side.

She couldn't feel his hand on her arm and her vision was covered with spots. Two spells seemed to be her limit right now. She stared at the road and waited for her vision to clear.

The shale on one side was gone. The rest of it remained

One would have to do. She allowed Lyle to pull her up and slid her arm over his shoulders before he led her to the palanquin. With a tired smile, she sank into the seat.

"I'm okay, you know."

"Ye don't look okay," he said bluntly. "Ye stay there and let me get us through this passage."

"Lunch first," she said decisively.

"While I'm all for lunch—"

"Lyle." She put a hand on his arm. "If I'm more alert, I may be able to sense threats in the same way I sensed the passage itself."

"Oh. Fair enough."

They ate a quiet meal and she remained somewhat dreamy from exhaustion. It was only at the end that she thought to look at Lyle, and her heart squeezed when she saw him staring sadly at the landscape. She wanted to reassure him but to her surprise, tears threatened.

Instead, she let him lead the horses through the tunnel and went through in the palanquin. The dwarf and one pony pushed ahead, followed by the pony dragging the palanquin and her horse at the back. The damp coolness of the tunnel helped, in some ways, to wake her.

It was also dark and cozy, however, which meant she had a nap or two in the darkness.

Like the other passage, it was long enough that they lost sight of all daylight for a time. Eventually, the smell of fresh air and the growing light told her they would soon emerge into the orcish lands.

When they did, at last, she was awoken from another nap by Lyle's exclamation. Dotty sat abruptly and peeked her head out of the palanquin.

It was immediately obvious what had caused his amazement. The trees were at least as big as the redwoods of California, large enough that one could make a tunnel through the center of one and drive a car through with sufficient space left on either side. They stretched so far that she only had the vague sense of green leaves and dappled sunlight.

For the forest was light. It was alive and filled with the calls of birdsong and the creak of the trees. Bushes growing in the spaces between the redwoods rustled and the very air seemed to be alive.

"It's *beautiful*." She felt the same kind of amazement she'd known when she first looked at the sea at night. Although entirely dwarfed by the landscape, it was enough to fill her with happiness.

The road, such as it was—it looked as disused on this side of the tunnel as it had on the other—wound into the forest without any markers. They set off in silence, both still entranced by the floating motes of dust and the flutter of birds and butterflies.

No settlements appeared for a long time, exactly like there had been no dwarven villages in the increasingly hostile landscape on the other side of the mountains. The ponies plodded onward, apparently unimpressed by the grandeur around them, and the two companions exchanged the occasional glance.

It wasn't a sense of being watched that left them wary. It was more that the longer they continued, the stranger it became that there were no people.

Finally, Dotty realized that she could smell smoke.

She scrambled out of the palanquin and onto the back of the horse and her gaze met the dwarf's. There were no screams but the smell was faint but unmistakable. It grew heavier as they progressed, more and more oppressive and with a trace of something else she could not name but nevertheless feared.

At last, they rounded a bend in the road and she put her hand to her mouth in horror.

Whatever had happened, there were no survivors. Every single house had been systematically put to the torch. A pile in the center of the town revealed bones and she pressed the back of her hand more firmly over her mouth. Someone had rounded the villagers up and...what?

She wanted to turn and leave. It took more than a minute for her to persuade herself to get off the horse and venture forth. The animal certainly had no intention to do so.

"Dotty." Lyle sounded almost panicked. "If we're wanderin' into a war..."

Although she heard him, she could not respond. She trembled violently as she studied the carnage—every house burned, the well blocked, and the bodies stacked so neatly. It was destruction, and yet…why? Something seemed wrong, not entirely in keeping with what she expected from a war.

She stopped dead a moment later. "This place…"

"Dotty, it may be best to leave if they're in the middle of a—"

"It wasn't a war," she said quietly. She turned to look at him. "It was a plague. This was the village I came from. *I* did this. I gave them the burial I could and I made sure no one would live here until it was safe again."

CHAPTER TWENTY-TWO

"Ye did this?" Lyle asked blankly.

"Yes. No." Dotty shook her head. "I told you my village had been destroyed by a plague. I was given the life of that person for a time and this is their history." She looked around. "These were her family and friends and she saw all of them die. She had to bury them alone."

He dismounted and came to join her. While she could see that he wanted to be anywhere but there, he came to stand with his friend. She smiled gratefully at him.

"Um." He cleared his throat. "Do ye...want t' bury them?"

"I..." She looked at them. "No. She gave them last rites according to their ways. We should leave this place in peace, I think. But—give me a moment?"

The dwarf nodded wordlessly and returned to the ponies.

She knelt on the rich ground of the forest floor, heedless of the gown, and looked at the ash mixed among the leaves. This village had seen so much fear and grief and the loneliness of one woman, the last of her kind, setting out with the pyre still smoldering.

And that young woman had died fighting a dragon only a few

weeks later. Had she heard that story from someone else, she would have thought it a tragic tale. The woman had survived for only a short while and had perhaps gone to her death because she could not face living without everyone she loved.

But she knew the story was very different—one of a woman who had triumphed against all odds and who had survived to bring justice to an entire race. That woman had not merely stoked rebellion and walked away. She had put herself into the fray and sacrificed her life before any other.

It was enough to make her wonder what other stories she thought she knew that might be not of loss but of hope and victory.

The faint tremble beneath her fingertips did not catch her attention at first. She felt tears on her cheeks, not least of all for Prima, who had lived this—every orc in this village suffering and dying of the plague. She hoped she had brought the AI some joy out of it. When the shaking grew louder, she recognized it for what it was—hoofbeats.

"Dotty!" Lyle was at her side and pulled at her arm, but it was too late to run.

The orcs were there.

"You." Their leader swung off her horse. She had greenish-brown skin and the lean build of a runner, and her muscles rippled as she walked. "Before you die for what you did here, you will tell me how you came to these lands."

Dotty stood with Lyle's help. She bowed as Rashat and Huwat had taught her.

"What happened here," she said clearly, "was a plague." She took a deep breath. "There was one survivor, a young woman named Dahti. She laid her people to rest and built the pyre, and then she set out to find a new home. She found one only for a short time in the village of Mountain's Shadow in the Fire lands. When their godspring awoke, she led them against it and sought the training of the legendary water shaman, Rashat, to defeat it.

The price of that victory was her life. I kneel here in memory of her."

The chieftain looked at her. "We have heard that story," she said. "But how do you know it?"

She closed her eyes for a moment. "I know it because she was given many lives," she said finally. "She lived two before she watched her village lost and she stands before you now. If you doubt me, as I can only assume you do, I ask you to bring me to Rashat and to Huwat and the people of Mountain's Shadow. There, I can share things I would know only from experience, things they will remember."

The orcs looked warily at one another, but the chieftain did not seek approval. She considered her and her alone.

"Come here," she said at last.

Lyle made a strangled kind of noise, but Dotty moved around the edge of the village and picked over tumbled fences and mud bricks. She had to work to keep her face straight as the smell of the orcs hit her.

She'd forgotten how bad it was.

"You tell me you are an orc," the woman said.

"I tell you that I have once been an orc," she said.

The chieftain looked halfway between annoyed and amused. "The story is too strange for me to believe it."

"I understand," she told her simply. "I do. I too would disbelieve it."

"And you want us to take you to Rashat," the orc said after a moment's thought.

"If you want proof, yes. But I also wish to speak to him on behalf of the city of Insea—him and the other leaders, yourself included."

"What a coincidence." The orc now looked anything but friendly. "One might almost think you knew what was happening—and, unless I miss my guess, you're a magic-wielder as well."

"I am," she said. "As to what is happening…I have my hopes but no knowledge."

"And you want me to risk our leaders by bringing an outsider into their midst?"

Dotty wondered how she could allay her fears. "Is there any way you would feel safe?"

The chieftain thought for a moment before she returned to her horse. She rummaged in the saddlebags and retrieved a single iron manacle, which she held up to her. "Block your magic and I will trust you enough to bring you to the shamans."

She held out one wrist in silence, even though she could practically feel Lyle's concern radiating at her. But she remembered, too, how Atra and the other young warriors of the water tribe had welcomed her once the shock of her appearance wore off.

The dwarf stepped beside her, and she feared that he might argue or make things worse. Instead, he murmured to one of the warriors, who in turn murmured to the chieftain. She looked at her.

"I am told you are ill and must ride in that…box."

She gave her friend a look that was exasperated and grateful in equal measure. If this would be a long trip, she would certainly need to rest.

"Yes," she admitted. "I am not well—a mass here, in my stomach. It will kill me soon."

The woman looked almost sympathetic for a moment but wiped the expression away quickly. "We will take you both," she said. "Go. Sit in your box. Your dwarf, too." She held a hand up. "Both of you will be blindfolded."

"For how long?" she asked.

She only shrugged. In the next moment, a blindfold came down over Dotty's eyes and she was led to the palanquin, stumbling over the leaves and sticks, and listened to the dwarf do the same—swearing profusely and inventively every step of the way, of course.

The orcs seemed to appreciate that, at least. She heard a few snickers at some of the more colorful invectives, and their handlers were more careful in helping them over obstacles as a result.

She had guessed that Lyle's straight-talking warrior mentality would appeal to many of the orcs, but it was still surprising to see it in action.

As the curtains closed around them, she leaned back with a sigh—only to realize that she had missed the post. She flailed to keep her balance and wound up kicking Lyle in some place that felt squishy.

"Lyle?"

"M'okay," the dwarf wheezed.

"Oh, no." She lowered her face into her hands. "I'm so sorry. No, no, don't try to respond," she added. "Well…I suppose this is going fairly well."

"Ye think this is going *well?*"

"Well, I didn't get kicked in the groin so that does color my perception somewhat."

"I *mean*," he said, "we're blindfolded an' bein' hauled into orc territory."

"That was where we were trying to go, though. So instead of wandering around looking for all the different shamans, they're *taking* us to them."

"I hadn't thought about it that way," he confessed. "Ye haven't got yer magic, though."

"It seems a reasonable precaution. I have killed more than one dragon. And some weird elf-thing in a black suit. And so on." She felt for the pillows more carefully this time, curled up, and yawned as soon as she rested her head. "I'm going to take a nap."

"How can ye sleep at a time like this?"

"What else is there to do?" she asked reasonably. "We seem to be safe and we can hardly be expected to navigate anything. Rest, Lyle."

He grumbled in response and she was fairly sure that, by the time they stopped for the evening, he had still not allowed himself to rest. The air around them seemed different somehow, and the wind freer—they must have left the forest—but other than that, she could not have said what direction they had gone in or where they were.

The next few days passed in much the same way. She learned several skills she had never wanted regarding balance and neatness while blindfolded but otherwise, had a pleasant enough journey. Despite the blindfold and certain clearly forbidden topics of conversation, their companions in the group were willing to speak to them and even laugh and exchange stories around the campfire at night.

Dotty was fairly sure that a number of stories were designed to test her story, which she accepted with good humor.

If someone had appeared in a cloth-of-silver gown and claimed to be a thrice-reincarnated hero of the American Revolution, for instance, she probably wouldn't have believed them in the slightest.

It was clear before long, however, that the surroundings had changed drastically. The air grew chill and the palanquin tilted. They must be entering the territory of the air tribe, but she did not want to say so to Lyle for fear of bringing down the wrath of their escort. It did not matter much, she decided and was simply something to say to break up the monotony of sitting in the carriage while they jolted along the road.

They heard the gathering long before they were close to it. The sound drifted eerily on the mountain wind, sometimes in snatches of song, sometimes in the beat of drums or the tramp of many feet. Dancing, making pilgrimage, or simply making their way up the mountain together? All were possible.

The din grew almost deafening before their caravan stopped. Shouts demanded that orcs get out of the way, followed by many hushed whispers.

Finally, the curtains of the palanquin were drawn back and she was pulled out. She swayed and covered her eyes in agony when the blindfold was removed. It had been so long since she had seen light and she forced herself to let it through in small amounts until at last, she could squint and look around.

Great, she thought acidly. Her first meeting with the council of shamans would be with her eyes streaming with tears, all bedraggled after days on the road, and her face screwed into a grimace.

But when her eyes did clear, she could have laughed. "Rashat! Huwat! *Atra!*"

What she did not expect was for Atra to step forward with a spear aimed directly at her chest. "Who are you?" the young woman demanded. "And how do you know our names?"

"The truth," Rashat added. His voice was as chill as deepest winter.

"I'm Dahti," she told them. "I fought with you and studied with you. We stayed at the village, you and I, after the rest of the tribe left to take shelter in the tunnels. We lured the godspring over the village fire to impale it on the spear. We traveled to face the godspring at Mountain's Shadow, and one life of mine passed there."

But he only shook his head. "Lies," he said, and his voice was even harder than it had been before. "Be honest, human, or we will kill you here and now."

CHAPTER TWENTY-THREE

This was not, Dotty had to admit, how she had thought this would go. There had been A Plan.

Also, things had gone so well. Yes, she had faced the displeasure of the dwarven council but she had found a solution. They had worked together.

Now, she was on a plateau in the middle of nowhere, surrounded by weapons and without her magic, and the one thing that should have worked—the truth—would almost certainly get her nowhere.

"May I speak to you alone?" she asked Rashat. She looked at Huwat. "Or you?"

"No."

She held her hand up to display the iron manacle. "I have no magic and I have no weapons. I mean you no harm—nor, let's be honest, could I do any if I wanted to." She looked meaningfully at the orcs. Compared to her, they were hulking.

"Fine," Rashat said. He swept an arm imperiously and the others stepped aside to allow their small procession into an ornate tent.

Inside, the two shamans took seats on the floor. She had not been invited to sit and decided not to chance her luck by doing so. Instead, she looked around and noted with alarm that Lyle was not here.

"Will the dwarf be safe?"

The water shaman's brow furrowed. "You have asked to speak to us. No emissaries would be harmed until negotiations were concluded."

That was not *precisely* heartening, but she didn't want to point that out.

"Speak," he said, clearly impatient.

"Is there anything I could say," she asked, "any question I could answer or any memory I could recall to convince you that I am telling the truth?"

They wanted to say no. She saw it in their eyes. It was the instinctive answer to her question.

"Believe me," she said, "if I could choose my story, I would not have chosen this one. I would simply have said I was an emissary."

Rashat chuckled unwillingly at that before he said, "Our last lesson—*the* last lesson—before the Godspring attacked. What happened?"

Dotty took time to think back. "We were walking to the village when it came from the depths," she said. "I had…called it—not on purpose but by using fire and earth magic when I sat in the sea. I was cold and trying to warm myself." Her eyes drifted closed. "That was days before, though. That night…I can't—oh. You had finally pushed me to the point where I fought back physically instead of only with magic. You wanted me to use magic only as one tool in my arsenal."

His brows raised. He schooled his face to impassivity a moment later and nodded to Huwat. "A question from you next."

The fire shaman was ready. "With what provisions did you go to the next tribe?"

"Mushrooms and root vegetables," she said at once. "They

were from the cave the shamans used for their rites. You intended to send me with more, but the village had run from their home and I told you to keep half."

Huwat nodded silently and looked at Rashat.

Dotty, meanwhile, resisted the urge to scream. She was her and they clearly knew it.

"How did you—how do you *claim* you came to be reborn?" the water shaman asked. "You are not a babe in arms as you by rights should be."

"How…" She struggled to find words. "That is a strange tale. In Insea, there is a tournament. One human fighter, who had come here from another world—in itself a story—won the final prize, a key that would take him home. He had seen the danger that threatened this world, and he promised he would come back and bring help. I am one of the people he brought, and it was only my spirit that came here, not my body as well." She smiled. "Which is as well, honestly. My old bones wouldn't have made this journey in good shape."

"You always did claim you had grandchildren," Rashat murmured. His brows snapped together. "But your story is well beyond the realm of reason. We must think on this—and also think what we wish to do. You and your dwarf—"

"He's not *my* dwarf," she protested.

He continued as if he hadn't heard her at all. "Will be confined to a tent and kept under guard," he said. "I advise you to not disobey orders. You will find that our people are strong and their commitment to the law is absolute."

She had witnessed the crumbling of certain orcish traditions and had personal thoughts on how absolute that commitment was, but she held her tongue. Instead, she smiled and said simply, "Thank you."

It wasn't long before she and Lyle were shut in another far less ornate tent.

"So…are they goin' t' execute us?" he asked as he unrolled his bedroll. "And what do we have for food?"

"Nothing yet—and that's still better than the dried fish they ate in the water tribe." She shuddered.

"Well, I'll tell ye one thing, they'd best not drink me ale."

"If it gets us a peace treaty…" She shrugged. "And no, I wouldn't say we're in immediate danger. I think they know I'm telling the truth. It's merely a rather awkward truth and it leaves them in a strange position."

"Huh." He plopped down, his expression disgruntled. "I wish we could go out. I hear dancin'."

"Once again, we were *specifically* cautioned against that." She sat as well. The palanquin was outside, but the furs and pillows from inside it were in with them now. "There's no need to have the one of us who *isn't* dying get killed by orcs."

"Ye don't have t' sell me on it," Lyle assured her. "I'm in no rush to die."

"Are you sure? Because I've heard many stories about you. Some of them are stories *you* told me."

"Eh." He dismissed the ambiguity with a shrug. "What's yer plan, then?"

Dotty sighed. "Eventually, given that they know who I am, I assume they'll hear me out. From there, it will simply be the matter of finding out what's going on in the orcish lands and making sure we can be allies—or, at least, friendly acquaintances."

"They don't seem very happy about outsiders," Lyle pointed out.

"Do you blame them? You said yourself that your people were a nightmare, and you've met the Elves. As for humans—"

"You, Tina, and Justin are enough to make that point," he said with a shudder.

"Hey!"

He grinned at her. "What d'ye think they'll want?"

"I haven't the faintest clue." She lay back and pillowed her head on her hands. Wind whistled around the tent, eerie even in the daylight, and filtered in only through the gaps between the shelter's sides. "The water tribe was almost destroyed, so perhaps they would want materials for rebuilding. I don't know very much about the other tribes and their needs, though."

"Ye sound worried."

"Wouldn't you be?"

"Eh." He shrugged. "Either we find something or they kill us. Ye're smart, so there's no point in worryin' about it."

"Ah." Dotty wasn't sure how much more of this confidence she could take. "So, how do you think the others are doing?"

"Ugh. They have their work cut out for them." Lyle sat now. "The human lords hate each other more than almost anything. They have so many grudges that if ye allied with one of 'em, even *he'd* be angry at you about it."

She burst out laughing. "Oh, dear," she said a moment later. "I shouldn't laugh, I shouldn't. But it's funny. Especially because I know Tina won't stand for any of that. She'll catch every one of those things that don't make sense."

"And bonk 'em over the head with it," he finished and nodded slowly.

"She does have a way with words."

"I wasn't speakin' metaphorically." He fished a pipe out of one of his many pockets. "Do you mind if I smoke?"

"No. Harry used to—my husband. Not many do nowadays and I miss it."

"Huh." He lit the pipe and puffed on it to get the flame going. "Maybe we should leave well enough alone. If they don't want to come out of their lands—"

"No." Dotty sat at that. "The world grows and changes, people push against their borders, technology continues—there's no way they'll stay isolated forever, even if they want to. The dragons kept them trapped for far too long, and I'd be willing to bet they stoked fears of the outside while they were at it."

"I hadn't considered that." Lyle looked at her. "Ye speak like ye know these things. *Were* ye a diplomat? Ye say no, but…"

"I come from a very different time." She managed a smile. "I'd say it's a more complicated one, but I remember my youth—every time and every world is complicated in its own way. It's easy to let nostalgia take hold."

She stood and began to pace, her arms wrapped around herself. Her gown, although it was not as ornate as the one she had worn in Berghold, was still not what one would call either serviceable or functional.

"If you want my guess," she said to him after a few minutes of pacing, "they'll open up. I don't know how long it will take. They'll choose to open up and after that, there'll be a ton of nostalgia for *this*—for the days when they were kept to their individual tribes by the dragons. People will forget how bad it was to have the beasts demanding sacrifices of the young warriors. Hell, they'll realize soon enough that coming together, all tribes at once, has problems too. But if they're lucky, things will still be better." She stopped and chewed on one thumbnail for a moment. "No, things *will* be better," she said. "I met the young of the water tribe. You should have seen their fire, Lyle—although I suppose that's an ironic way to put it."

The dwarf laughed.

"They'll fight to make their world better," she told him. "And they *will* make it better."

Dotty settled on the furs, her heart less heavy with fear. It was only then that she saw the tent flap move slightly and fall into place.

Who had been listening? She stared at the makeshift door and her heart pounded. What would they think of what they had heard?

The two companions waited while the light faded and the

sounds outside changed to eating, accompanied by the smell of roasted vegetables and meat and fresh-baked bread. A guard brought them food with a sympathetic look and a great deal of curiosity.

The meal was doubtless composed of leftovers, but both were too hungry to care. They wolfed it down and fell asleep listening to the sounds of dancing and music.

In the middle of the night, she was woken with a knife at her throat and warm breath at her ear.

"Come with me," Atra said quietly. "Make a single sound, though, and I will kill you."

CHAPTER TWENTY-FOUR

Jamie and Emilia ran, shrieking, through a field of long grass.

"They could be kids again," Simon said ruefully. "If you discounted the weapons, that is." He took his glasses off and rubbed the bridge of his nose. When he spoke a moment later, he did not look at his wife. "What are we going to do?"

Aimee leaned back in her chair. The PIVOT team had set aside a private conference room for them where they could watch Jamie and Emilia's progress through the game and speak in privacy.

Finally, she said, "I don't think we have a choice. Do you?"

"No," he admitted and smiled at the screen. "*They* certainly made their feelings clear. You know, I was proud of them for saying it."

"Be proud without giving them big heads," she advised.

His smile broadened. Even after twenty-two years with this woman at his side, he was still delightedly taken aback every time one of her Southern grandmother's platitudes came out of her mouth. Her accent grew stronger when she said those things.

She knew and nudged him with an elbow. "Still? Two decades

and you still think it's funny to see a Chinese woman with a Southern drawl?"

"I met you in New York," he said with a helpless shrug. "It was a very important moment for me and I will *always* expect you to have a New York accent and…New York parenting advice."

"What would that be?" Aimee asked him precisely. "Never sit in the last subway car? Don't trust hot dog vendors?"

Simon laughed.

Her smile had slipped from her face, though. "I don't want them to think they run the show," she said quietly. "If they push for this, we agree, and something happens to her…"

"It'll be no more dangerous than waiting for it to get worse on its own," he said.

"I know that. But emotions don't. They'd feel guilty for the rest of their lives." Aimee took a deep breath and shook her head. "I've been over every moment of my pregnancy, it feels like, and her first weeks. Did I pay more attention to Jamie, did I eat something wrong—"

"*My love.*" Aghast, he swung his chair to face her. "Have you wondered that all these years?"

She didn't look at him. Instead, she had her hands pressed between her knees and she was shaking. "Yes."

"Aimee. Love. Please look at me." He tried to take one of her hands but she was like a statue. Instinct told him that if he moved her, she would crumble—and she so hated to do so in public. He placed his hand gently on her leg. "I saw you with every one of our children. I saw you when you were pregnant. Whatever dark moments you had, if you were exhausted or even angry, if you spoke to them harshly, that is what it means to be *human.* If something like that could cause this, every child on earth would have what Taigan has." Cautiously, he tried a joke. "At least then they'd probably have a cure for it."

Her chin trembled and he thought he'd made a terrible mistake, but then she started to laugh. She was crying too, and tears poured down her face as she clasped his hands while she leaned her forehead against his.

"Why didn't you tell me?" Simon whispered. His heart was breaking at the thought that his wife had spent years fearing she was at fault.

The laughter took a moment to settle, but her face crumpled with tears. "I was afraid you'd agree," she whispered. "And that you'd—"

"Never." He wrapped an arm around her. "Taigan could not have a better mother."

Her eyes drifted closed and she shook her head.

"Yes, Aimee."

"No. Because what about *them*?" She gestured to the screen where Emilia and Jamie were still playing—more playing tag than doing any kind of quest if the truth be told. "You saw how angry Emilia was. There wasn't enough time for everything."

"We did the best we could." His heart would break more than once during this conversation, he realized. "It wasn't enough and it wasn't what they should have had. But no parents could have done this perfectly, Aimee. When they're older, they'll know that. I think they even know it now. And we can do better."

She took a deep breath and raised her hand to touch his cheek. "But the best way to do better," she said, "*really* do better… is if Taigan is cured."

"You know," he told her after a moment, "I don't think *this* was what my father warned me about when he said, 'you get married and suddenly, your wife is always right.' But he was right."

Aimee flicked him lightly on the knee and laughed. "Your father, I swear."

"He did like you, you know." He kissed her.

"Uh-huh." She sighed and rubbed her face. "So we're doing this again. All the transfer paperwork, finding someplace to stay… It never gets easier. Why doesn't it get easier?"

"It does sometimes," Simon said. "There's AirBnB now."

"Okay, that's true." She raised one eyebrow mischievously. "Dibs on finding a place to stay."

"*No.* I demand a rematch."

"I don't make the rules." She grinned.

Simon laughed and took her hands. "So, we're doing this. We are doing this. *Wait.*" He stood. "I want to do something. Tell me your memories of Taigan. Tell me things you saw her do—wait, pairs of things. A thing you saw her do, and a thing you did when you were her age."

She smiled. "Ah… Hmm. I did love the way she always dressed up. Emilia and Jamie were so careful during their games—they had to have the pirate hat to play pirate games or whatever, but Taigan would put on any old thing and run off. Do you remember the time she took my pearls and said she was a dinosaur?"

"I remember we pulled the pearls out of the fish pond later," he said, laughing. "And the second part?"

"Ah, hmmm. The second part. Well, I suppose someday, I hope we see her wearing a beautiful pearl necklace of her own." Aimee smiled. "Maybe at a wedding? Or a…graduation?" Her voice broke slightly but she smiled. "Your turn, before I cry."

"Well, you've got me there. I proposed the game but I didn't have anything." He leaned against the table and thought hard. "I still love how she would cuddle in our laps when we read."

She smiled at the memory. "She always got around bedtime with that."

"'One more story, one more story,'" Simon said, quoting his daughter's almost constant refrain from ages two to six. "She knew we couldn't say no to that."

"Clever girl," Aimee agreed. "And what's the thing you want to see?"

"Hmm, what was I doing at seventeen? Nothing worthwhile, I can tell you that. I looked forward to having a place of my own, I guess. I'd like her to be able to walk into an empty apartment with boxes of her things and feel that total exhilaration, you know? That it will be your first time being on your own but it's all yours to shape."

"That's a good one." She laced her fingers through his.

"Your turn again."

"Again? Hmm. I love how when she did gymnastics, she could never quite stick the landing because she was so proud of herself—she wanted to rush over to us for a hug." She smiled. "Although it was sometimes exasperating. As for memories of me at seventeen…oh." Her face went still.

"What is it?"

"I want her to have her heart broken," she said and looked at him. "I don't want her to be in pain—not *that* part of it—but to know that the pain can't break her and she can be happy on her own. I worry that she'll never let herself get close to someone because of this. And if she does, I worry she'll be too scared to let the relationship go if she needs to."

"Now that you mention it, that was part of being seventeen for me, too." He sighed. "It's amazing what the passage of thirty years can do for perspective. At the time, I wanted to cry my eyes out—not that my father would have allowed it—and beg for her to come back and maybe put my fist through a wall."

"You? Really?"

"Seventeen is a rough age. Give me a break." He uttered a rueful laugh. "But the thought of never meeting you—that's horrifying."

Aimee squeezed his fingers. "Heartbreak is like falling and skinning your knees, hmm? It's part of learning to be a person. Your turn. Then I suppose we should tell them what we mean to do."

"Probably." Simon kissed her. "I love the way she never sang the same tune as everyone else. She was always trying to harmonize. Then she got *too old and dignified* to sing grace, of course." He shook his heads. "Kids. And…I want her to go grocery shopping for the first time and come home and realize how many things she's missing. It's not funny when you try to cook a meal, but it's part of the process."

She laughed, stood, and pulled him up. They kissed and shared the silence that had been so much a part of their lives—silence with the beeps of medical equipment, silence as they drove to yet another facility, or the silence of a night in a strange house.

They had learned to speak to one another simply with silence. And now, both of them looked at the screen, where their other two children still played and laughed. As they stood there, Simon and Aimee decided another thing in silence.

They sat together to watch. They would transfer Taigan to PIVOT soon and there would be the mountain of paperwork and the trials of deciding where the kids would stay and who would shuttle back and forth.

But right now, they had a moment to watch their children play and they wouldn't pass it up. Because they were rebuilding the family for all of them, not only Taigan.

CHAPTER TWENTY-FIVE

Atra led her around the edge of the campground. Cloaked in darkness, they wove between silent tents and orcs slumbering beneath the night sky. When Dotty looked up, amazed by a completely unfamiliar night sky, a prick of the knife reminded her to keep walking.

It was impossible to ignore that they were drawing closer and closer to the edge of the plateau.

At last, they reached a statue, a pillar made of metals, stone, and wood. It reminded her of a mosaic, although she had never seen a column done this way and there was no picture she could see. Each piece of it had a carving, and although she wanted to see them more closely, she did not dare. This place felt holy, surrounded by dozens upon dozens of low-guttering candles.

She glanced at Atra, whose gaze was fixed on the pillar. The orc was steeling herself in preparation for something.

Please, let it not be her murder. They were so high above the plains below. It must be hundreds of feet down and her heart clenched at the thought of falling and of the pain.

"Atra…" she began.

"Stop." The warrior's words were more measured than she

expected. "You stand in the presence of gods—our true gods, the old gods. Know that in this place, they can hear every lie you speak."

Understanding dawned and with it, hope.

She inclined her head. "I swear to you, I will speak no lie in this place."

"*Who are you?*"

"I am Dotty. I am a woman with four children and with grandchildren and great-grandchildren. I am dying from a mass in my stomach. This is the third time I have come to this world, and it will be the last. The first time, it was as a dwarven woman. The second time, it was as the orc you met, Dahti. The third, you see before you."

"Still you lie," Atra whispered. Her head shook and she held the knife out so it gleamed under the stars.

Dotty could sense something else beneath the surface, but she could not grasp it. "Why do you say so?" Then, fumbling her way to the truth, she asked, "Why do you *need* for this to be a lie, Atra?"

The woman's lip curled in a snarl. "You know nothing about me."

"I know some things." She looked steadily at her. "I know you were trained to defend your people and you could easily have killed me the first time we met. I know your grandmother is one of the elders of the tribe and you brought me to her, knowing she would disapprove but *also* knowing that the traditions of the tribe allowed it. I know you once asked Rashat why he was always sad."

Atra's eyes looked like pools of black in the darkness. "No," she whispered.

"Atra." Dotty stepped forward and regretted it immediately when the woman's face closed off. Desperately, she held her hands out. "I was your ally once. I sacrificed my life for your people. Surely you heard that story from Rashat."

"You convinced us to kill our gods," the warrior hissed, "to go against our traditions, and you had *no right*. You came to us cloaked in the skin of our people. You pretended to be one of us, but you never were."

"Atra, your shamans agreed that the gods were unjust."

"Because you came to whisper in their ears!" Atra clapped a hand over her mouth as her voice rose. She looked around, fearful that she had woken the others. "You *had no right*. It was our injustice to right. They were our traditions to keep or throw away."

Dotty looked down. Her head was reeling.

She had given her life to protect these people and to warn them that their ways were slowly killing them. How *dare* Atra say this to her? Anger pumped hot through her veins.

For the first time, she doubted why she was there. Prima was her friend, and Lyle, but she had counted Atra among her friends, too. She had wanted to leave a world in which the young woman could be happy and, as Lyle had pointed out, she had her world to think about too.

If this was the reaction she would get, shouldn't she have simply stayed in her world?

Lord knew, there were injustices there too.

Disheartened, she turned away to look over the plateau and the people sleeping in their huddles and tents. In the dark, there was no telling who was from which tribe. There were only orcs—hundreds of them and perhaps thousands.

The representatives of each tribe.

"Have you nothing to say for yourself?" Atra asked.

Her anger, which had faded while she watched the sleeping gathering, came back with a vengeance.

"No," she said shortly. "I have no apologies to make. I came to help and I *did* help, and I risked my life to do so—and gave it, not sure there would ever be another incarnation. You have no right to judge me." She leaned forward. "And if you think to kill me now, know that it will not help you. When the orcs reach out, they can find allies or they can find those who do not care for them at all. Kill me and you will assure the latter."

"The orcs never need to go beyond our borders," the woman retorted, hatred in her tone. "We have enough to do rebuilding what you tore down."

Dotty turned and left before she could say something she would regret.

She was several tents away and moving farther into the camp before she realized that she did not know where she was—and that she was now in defiance of Rashat's orders. Frustrated, she looked at the sleeping orcs and closed her eyes for a moment in defeat.

Stupidly, she wanted to cry. She had come to help and they didn't want that. They couldn't see how she had already helped them. She forced herself to overcome the tears and through her blurred gaze, caught sight of the main tent. Quickly, she picked her skirts up and hurried toward it. From there, she could find her bearings, return to Lyle, and hatch a plan to get out of here.

Except that, as she approached it, a tall shape pushed the door aside and stepped out.

Dotty skidded to a halt and swallowed.

"Why are you out alone?" Rashat asked her.

"Because one of yours took me to the edge of the plateau and threatened my life," she told him as coldly as she could muster.

"Atra," he guessed at once.

"Yes."

"The girl has more anger than is good for her. Still...I might know something about that." He looked at her. "And if you're as old as you claim, you must know the same."

She gritted her teeth. "I didn't throw the accomplishments of my elders in their faces."

"Didn't you?" he asked, genuinely amused. "What a strange young one you must have been. I didn't, of course. But that's because they were almost all dead." He held a hand out and gestured in the direction from which she had come. "Walk with me. I would show you something."

"If it's the cliff, believe me, I've seen it," she told him. "I know how far down it is."

"Not that. Woman, if I wanted you dead, I'd kill you. Same as you with me. Do you think I don't know you can get out of that iron bracelet if you want?"

A little startled, she clutched her wrist in her other hand and realized he was right. The manacle was made for orcs and it was loose enough to slide her hand through. She nodded.

In silence, she walked with him through the campground. When she heard orcs stir in their sleep, she wasn't worried that they would wake and kill her. She could discern the scents of incense and the patterns on blankets and tents.

To her amusement, Rashat had brought her to the same pillar. She wanted to look around to see if Atra still lingered but she forced herself to remain still. Let Atra hear this, whatever was coming she thought as she studied her companion, who gazed up at the pillar.

"So much has been lost," he said quietly.

Dotty lowered her head and bit her lip.

"Each tribe brings a piece for each of their members," he said. "Beneath this layer of stones lies another and another. Every one of our people is counted here."

She looked up sharply in amazement. "Truly?"

"What did you think a gathering of tribes was for?" Rashat asked wryly. "We are here to take an accounting of our strengths. This is one of the few traditions we can remember, and it is because one of the air tribe found a pillar inscribed with names." He paused. "But so many of our traditions had no monuments. They are songs that are gone from memory, the names of gods we never knew, and the stories of our ancestors…"

His voice faded. In the distance, a dying fire popped and hissed.

"We took it from ourselves," he said.

Another silence followed and Dotty decided to try speaking.

"Don't you think there are perhaps things you've done in the past centuries that are worth keeping as *new* traditions in spite of everything?" She narrowed her eyes at his expression. "What is it?"

"You still do not see," he told her.

She looked at the pillar, then to the edge of the plateau, and finally, behind her.

"It is not a thing you can see with your eyes," the shaman said impatiently. "One might almost think you were being purposefully dense."

"I didn't come here to be insulted and threatened." She glared at him.

"No," Rashat said. "You came to secure something from us, did you not?"

This was a dangerous path and she swallowed cautiously. "And to give something in return. Something you *need*."

"Oh?" He smiled. "And what is that?"

"Alliances," she said fiercely. "When you venture beyond these lands—"

"Who says we will?"

"The world has changed," she told him. "D'you remember what the godspring said in the fire village—that one of his kind had died to give the world peace? I've found the origins of that story since we last spoke, and the godspring did not lie. Peace was held for generations by the dwindling life of one dragon and now, he is dead and the world is beginning to descend into chaos. Who can say how much of your desire to stay here was due to that spell? And how much that spell contributed to the fact that no one came into your lands?"

The shaman looked genuinely surprised. "I admit, I had not considered that the worm was telling the truth."

She shrugged. "The world always seems to be stranger than we expect."

"And so you came to bring us alliances we need," he said slowly. "That is why?"

"Yes."

"You are lying. You came to gain an alliance because this new world threatens you more than it does us. It is because you do not want us to sweep off the plains and conquer your towns."

"It does not matter if you conquer them," she said without thinking. "War devastates all, no matter who wins."

"True enough."

"How would you know?"

"Because my tribe faced the water dragon twice," he said coldly. "And does it seem to you that we were *victors* in that exchange?"

Dotty bit her tongue and nodded. He had a point.

"So you have lied to us about why you came. You were a petitioner who didn't come out of altruism but out of self-interest."

"Can it not be *both*?" she cried finally. Even though she heard others begin to wake at the sound of their exchange, she did not stop. She wanted them to hear her. "I'm not of Insea and I'm not of the orcs, but I want to help them. I want to know that when I leave, I leave a world at peace. Why do you mistrust me so?"

He was not at all swayed by her words and had expected them, she could see that.

"Because you want to save us," he told her. "You came to a place where you did not belong and tried to save us from ourselves and our gods. Now, you come to try to save us from what you assure us will be a ruinous war. But you have no understanding of our past and don't know what wars there might have been. You do not know what *we* want, and you do not care."

Her jaw dropped at the accusation. First Atra and now Rashat.

And she knew, with a sickening twist in her stomach, that they were right.

It wasn't the whole of the story, of course, but they were right. *Now* she saw what Atra had been saying. When had she become stronger by having someone else solve her problems? When had her children?

But she had tried to do so for the orcs. She had wanted so badly to finish her life by doing some good in the world that she had forgotten the people who would live on and that they should choose. She bowed her head.

"What *do* you want?" she asked him finally.

He looked at the pillar as he spoke. "I want to reclaim what was lost," he said. "That is the first thing. Now, come. I will bring you back to your tent."

CHAPTER TWENTY-SIX

When Dotty woke the next morning, Lyle was shaking her urgently.

"Hmm?" She opened her eyes to the taste of metal in her mouth and an ache in her stomach. She blinked, half-sure that she would see the doctors when she opened her eyes again but it was still the dwarf. "What is it?"

"They're summoning us." He helped her sit and crouched to look in her eyes. "Ye don't look well."

"It's okay. I'm fine." She gestured for him to stand and help her up as well. She stumbled slightly when she stood and her head spun. "Give me a moment to have water and fix my hair and I'll be out." When he didn't move, she smiled. "Only a moment alone? Please?"

He hesitated but nodded and pushed the tent flap aside. Outside, she could hear him speak to the guards in low tones. She waited for them to come inside and demand her presence, but they did not.

Alone, she pressed her hand against her stomach and looked at the floor. She was dimly aware of Prima rebraiding her hair, but the AI did not speak.

"How bad is it?" she said finally.

"I don't know," Prima admitted. *"I don't have access to any of your bloodwork information. You're not...like Lyle. I can't see all of you."* She paused while her gown changed to one of deep blue. *"You don't feel well, do you?"*

"No." She swallowed. "And I don't want to...miss saying good-bye, you know? To my family. But if I'm okay, I don't want to ruin this, either."

"I'll put an alert out to the team," Prima said. *"I'll tell them to pull you out if they need to but if you're healthy enough, to leave you in. Would that work?"*

"Yes." She felt a rush of relief. "Thank you, Prima. Thank you so much."

"Thank you," the AI said quietly. *"Now, go. Lyle is worrying. I'll make sure you have better food tonight."*

Dotty left, her lips twitching. Prima liked to claim that certain events could not be altered and perhaps that was true—but she seemed perfectly capable of implanting suggestions in people's minds. Suggestions like, "Why don't you give Dotty some cake?"

She walked to the main tent and tried not to squint in the bright sunshine, while Lyle cast looks at her every few seconds from beneath bushy eyebrows.

"I'm all right," she told him after the fourth look. "I won't keel over, I promise. I merely woke up last night and had trouble getting back to sleep."

It was true, mostly.

"Have ye thought over what yer going to say?" he asked in a low voice.

"Yes." She had woken feeling ill but with the answer in her mind. "But *don't* muck it up by getting all annoyed."

"This should be good."

"Do you promise?" she asked him.

"Will you screw the dwarves over?"

"Hmm—don't look at me like that. I'm trying to decide if you'd think it was screwing them over. I don't think so."

"How reassuring."

The guards tried not to listen but didn't seem successful. Their expressions of interest confirmed this. They held the tent flaps back, their lips twitching, and the two were ushered into the relative darkness of the main tent.

It was filled to capacity. All the chieftains were there, including the woman who had found them at the earth tribe village. She acknowledged her with a nod. At her side was her tribe's shaman and all the other shamans were there as well. There was little in the way of regalia and it seemed the shamans and the chieftains wore the same loose, serviceable clothing as their villagers.

Dotty looked around, located Huwat in the crowd, and gave him a small smile. He nodded, although he tried to keep his face straight.

She did not see Atra.

"Emissaries," Rashat said. "Yesterday, we spoke to the human. Dwarf, tell us your story."

This was not what she had expected, and from the look on Lyle's face, it wasn't what he had expected, either.

He swallowed. "Er…"

The orcs waited. To their credit, not one of them laughed.

"I'm the son of a councilor in Berghold," he said. "A…chieftain, I guess you'd say. I might have been one meself, but I never liked th' idea o' sittin' around an' arguin' all the day long. As soon as I was old enough, I left an' hired meself out as a guard fer caravans an' such. I saw a lot o' places." He thought for a moment. "I fought a demon once," he added lamely.

Dotty tried desperately not to laugh. "That's generally not considered a footnote," she muttered.

"Ah," he said.

Rashat also looked as if he tried not to laugh. "And how did you come to be here?" he asked.

"After one o' my jobs—well, soon after the demon one, actually—I decided t' go home. Berghold had some problems I wanted to address." The dwarf hunched his shoulders. "I did some o' that but not much. When Insea needed emissaries…." He shrugged. "Among dwarves, ye can stake yer family's honor on a deal like this—bring a deal back to Berghold. What they wanted t' give the dwarves was good. So I did. Now we're here."

"So you function both as a representative of the dwarves and as a representative of Insea?" The water shaman arched one eyebrow.

"No, sir. Ye'll know when ye get a *real* representative from Berghold, as ye'll die of old age afore they finish gettin' to the point."

A round of snickers followed his declaration. Dotty felt both pride and annoyance. She had been right that he would get on well with the orcs and she should have simply let him handle things from the start.

Well, what was done was done.

"And would you stake your family's honor, likewise, on this human's word here?" Rashat asked him bluntly.

The dwarf nodded. "I would, sir. Not everyone will leave happy, I'll tell ye that now, but she'll be fair and she'll be honorable."

Her heart clenched and she looked at him. "Lyle—"

"Woman, d'ye honestly think I'd let myself be taken blindfolded through orc territory if I didn't trust ye?"

She blinked and pressed her lips together. She nodded wordlessly, rather afraid that if she spoke, she would either laugh or cry.

"Very well," Rashat said. He nodded at Lyle, then at her. "Tell us what Insea offers."

"And tell us," rumbled one of the chieftains, "what Insea *is*."

"That's somewhat complicated," Dotty said. She sketched the popular telling of Insea's history, including the fact that the king had never been seen and that the elves were creating a new monarchy. "Insea has never stood against any other nation in war, but neither has it cultivated allies. While the world becomes less peaceful, Insea believes that the only way to maintain the peace that has so enriched us is to strengthen the bonds between cities."

"So," the woman next to Huwat said, "when times were good, you did not seek allies but now you do to save yourselves."

"Yes," Dotty said bluntly.

Lyle sucked his breath in.

Dotty and the woman stared at each other and she smiled at the orc. "What is gone and past cannot be changed, but what is in the future can be."

Rashat tapped his staff on the ground twice and all focused on him. "You do not tell the whole truth, emissary. If you wish my support in these proceedings, you will tell it."

Now, she hesitated but she was committed. She had made her choice.

It was not the choice Jaco would have made, but it was the choice *she* made.

"If the truth can destroy something," she murmured to herself, "then it deserves to fall." Determined, she raised her chin. "Insea's peace was maintained without the knowledge or consent of its citizens by the life force of a dragon—kin of those who called themselves your gods. It bound the minds of the people inside the city and outside it as well so that they could not even have thoughts of war or violence against it. It was a peace based on trickery and subjugation, and the dragon's death has freed Insea of that trickery. Now, however, the city lies unprotected."

She knew what she was offering and she could see in their eyes how tempting it was. Then, to her surprise, the greed she saw there began to dissipate. The hunger left and the orcs nodded and settled.

"Insea was in chains, you say?" Huwat asked her. "Every citizen?"

"Everyone," she confirmed. "Leaders of other nations forgot their grudges and never sent their forces against the city. Now that the dragon is dead, there is only the populace. There are warriors among them and enough industry to power a war machine if need be—but who prospers in a war?"

"Mercenaries," Lyle said promptly.

"*Lyle.*"

"Oh, right. Sorry."

"We have seen the same," one shaman said after a time. He looked at the others. "We too were at peace, were we not? But it was not a true peace. That is gained through alliance."

"And peace," Dotty added, "is far, far more difficult than war. Do you think it is difficult to go onto a battlefield? It is more difficult to swallow your pride. I do not pretend that what comes next will be easy. I am simply a woman who has seen war far too often."

They looked at one another, but Rashat held her gaze. "What, then, do you offer us as the first token of friendship?" he asked her.

"Tools," she said. "Tools to help you recover what was lost. I offer the services of the *zauberers* of the dwarves and the wizards of the human realms. Much has been built since the tribes were scattered and much has been lost, but we will help you reclaim what you can."

He did not smile. Instead, she saw his shoulders settle as if a weight had been lifted from him. His eyes were closed and his face twisted as if almost in pain.

"And trade?" one of the chieftains asked her.

"Trade is a matter for if and when the orcs decide to open their borders," she said. "I have yet to see a nation that has not done so, but who can say what you will need or want at that time? Until that day, Insea will wait—here, if you wish or outside your borders if you would prefer."

Silence dragged on for a long while.

A thought occurred to her. "Are there still dragons you need help killing?"

"No," Rashat said mildly. "We took care of the problem."

The very blandness of it was chilling. Beside her, Lyle muttered, "Orcs. I tell ya."

She could only agree.

"So you have listened, then," the water shaman told her. "At last."

"I'm stubborn." She smiled at him. "But not *that* stubborn." She swayed slightly on her feet and realized she hadn't eaten since she woke up. A little desperately, she dug her nails into her palm and tried not to sway too obviously.

"We have heard your proposal," Rashat said formally after seeking out the gaze of each chieftain and shaman in the room. "We will discuss it amongst ourselves." His words spoke like a diplomat, careful to avoid promises, but his eyes told her that her suggestion had met with approval.

Peace. She wanted to laugh she was so relieved. But the room seemed to go dark at the edges—or were those spots dancing in her vision? She was aware of them only after the fact.

"Dotty?" Huwat stood.

"I'm…" But the world tipped, and as she fell, her last thought was, *I promised Lyle I wouldn't do this.*

Dotty is worried that she is unwell. She requests that she be taken out of the game in time to say goodbye to her family in person. However, if she is well enough, she would like to finish the mission.

Jacob stared at the email with a sense of gathering dread.

The AI that ran PIVOT's game should not have access to email. He hadn't set up any kind of way for this to happen. Somehow, it had moved beyond its network and was able to send messages.

He stood quickly. His palms were clammy and he smoothed them down his sides while his fingers shook. He wasn't entirely sure what he needed to do about this, and the only thing his mind could latch onto was that Dotty didn't feel well and her family should be called if her status was becoming critical.

When he heard the machines, he was halfway to the stairs. His mind reminded him that he heard them because everyone else had gone deathly silent.

In all honesty, he knew very little about medical machines. Still, he knew the noises these usually made and the tempo at which they made them. This was not normal. His mind gratefully freed itself from the predictions of a post-apocalyptic wasteland overrun with robots and latched onto the fact that something was wrong in the lab.

That was the kind of crisis he could do something about.

With renewed focus, he hurried down the stairs and around the corner to see people gathered around Dotty's pod. Aimee and Simon Mattis, who had been brought down for their children to be taken out of the game, held one another and looked shocked as almost every medical assistant swarmed around the other hub.

The two medical assistants who *did* remain—those who were assigned to first-line-of-oversight for Emilia and Jamie, respectively—looked immensely upset that they weren't able to see what was going on.

Jacob located Amber and Nick and hurried to them. They must have been in the process of having lunch because Nick held half a sandwich and Amber a fork. Both of them were tense and she bounced on the balls of her feet. She looked over at the sound of Jacob's footsteps.

"Thank God. I left my phone in the other room and I didn't want to…" She nodded toward the Mattises and lowered her voice. "I didn't want to yell that we had a problem. Someone should talk to them."

"Before we do that, what's going on?" He wasn't particularly worried about the Mattises seeing this and being ignored. What they needed to know was that it was being taken seriously.

"Dotty's status has…" She pressed her lips together and looked like she was about to cry.

"She's going into organ failure," DuBois said crisply. "I've called in her primary care physician, with whom she left very extensive instructions, and we're waiting to see what she wants to do."

"She wants to come out to say goodbye to her family in person," he told him.

Everyone swung to look at him except DuBois, who waved

one hand behind his back and snapped his fingers to get his attention. "How do you know that?"

"It's an automated alert she had set up," he said. "It goes to my email." He ignored the suspicious looks from his partners. "When her doctor gets here, let me know—and I'll call the family anyway. They need to know to stay near their phones, I think."

"You're right," Amber murmured. She swallowed hard. "I can't…I didn't think it would be this hard."

"She's doing very well," DuBois said.

"She is?" Everyone huddled closer.

"In the *game*," the doctor said, his expression long-suffering. "She's doing well in the *game*."

The group drew back with various noises of disappointment.

"Did you honestly think the cancer would magically go away?" he asked them.

"HIPAA," Amber reminded him sharply with a head-jerk toward the Mattises.

"Oh. Right. Sorry. Nothing." He returned to his work.

"I'll go talk to them," Amber told Jacob. "But how did you know about Dotty? And the truth this time."

"I…will tell you later." He shook his head. "It's a long story. And you know who we should also tell—Tina and Justin. I'll go handle that."

He walked away before she could ask him any more awkward questions.

Justin and Tina stared at the room with total weariness.

It was a paradise. The bed had to be twice the size of a king bed, if not larger, and it was covered with truly gorgeous silk bedding and hung with brocade curtains. Along one side was a personal library with comfortable chairs. Liquor in every color from pale gold to ruby was displayed in crystal bottles, a fireplace emitted the perfect amount of coziness, and the immensely tall windows looked out onto perfectly maintained gardens. From behind a folding screen, a curl of steam hinted at a warm bath.

But this was the tenth perfect room. This was the tenth night that they had been told there would be a feast in their honor.

Feasts and hotel rooms were fun for the first few nights, but after this much time, all he wanted was takeout and a movie. He wanted to wear sweatpants and play video games.

The irony hit him a moment later. He looked at Tina.

"Bleh," she said. She swung her arm tiredly to drop her bag and kicked it apathetically across the floor. "Do you have any idea how tired I am of fancy gowns? I want sweats."

"That's what I was thinking," he said. "Do you think we could skip the banquet tonight?"

"God, I fucking *wish*." She took a moment to summon her energy and made a flying leap onto the bed, where she landed sprawled out. "Oh, yeah," she said, her voice muffled by the blankets. "This is the stuff."

"Don't lie down or you won't want to get up again," he warned her.

"The damage is done. Go on without me."

"The hell I will. If I have to attend another feast and listen to them toast me and insult each other, so do you."

"Nope." She shook her head vigorously. "I can't do it. Won't. I swear to God, if I thought I could get past those guards with any kind of meaningful excuse, I'd be gone in a shot."

"Uh-huh." Justin grasped one of the bags and opened it. "Huh. Uh, Tina?"

"What?"

"Tina. Sit up. Look."

"Nope."

"*Tina.*" He clambered onto the bed and rolled her forcibly onto her side.

"Whoa, what the fuck is *that?*" She stared at the blue square hovering in the middle of the room. "I swear to God if this thing blue-screen-of-deaths while we're *in* it—oh, look, someone's typing."

"Dotty is not in good shape," Justin read as the words scrolled across the screen. "If you would like to say goodbye to her, we will try to arrange that. Get somewhere remote."

They looked at one another. Then, without a word, they snatched their bags up and hurried to the door. Without a word, they pushed past curious guards and raced to the main stairways and freedom.

"Prima, can you make sure there are horses ready?" he whispered as they barreled down a huge flight of stairs.

"I can. However, I should inform you that if you want to avoid company—"

"No time!" Tina called. She plastered a smile on her face. "Oh, hello, Lord…uh…my lord. Terrible problem with my cousin's nephew's wife's sister's great-aunt…very urgent."

"Diplomatic emergency," he added as the two of them sprinted to the stables.

"But the feast—" the lord called after them.

"I wish we could stay!" Tina responded over her shoulder. "I'm sure we'll be back!" Under her breath, she added, "When there's a cold day in hell."

In the stables, they danced with impatience while they waited while the horses that had only just been brushed were saddled. They scrambled to tie the saddlebags in place. Justin watched Tina's face and the somewhat manic concentration there.

"Are you okay?"

"Nope," she said flatly. "And I don't think I will be for a while. But I'd rather be out there and alone before I start bawling."

He nodded once and could feel the lump in his throat. If he tried to talk about this, he would also be a wreck.

For now, he simply had to hold himself together.

But his hand found hers and the two of them grasped each other's fingers until the bones ached.

Jaco signed his name on the last sheet of paper and flexed his hand. Both his hands ached, his back ached, and he was fairly sure someone had poured sand in his eyes and throat in the last hour.

He had been angry when Dotty signed over so many rights and could admit that. In his heart of hearts, he had hoped that the emissaries would manage fairly unilateral peace treaties that would not necessitate the truth coming out.

Of course, he had also known it would never work but he had still hoped. Dotty's bargain, the first to reach him, had been beyond fair. The terms she had negotiated would enrich both Insea and Berghold and truly *would* foster strength.

But Jaco would have to find a way to explain to the citizens of Insea that there was no king, there had never been a king, and that their centuries-long peace had been bought at great cost and with many lies.

More than anything, he was afraid the rebel elves would move in before he had time to make peace with them. He hadn't lived in Insea before Gos'hauke summoned him, but he had formed a close bond with the city and its people.

And he did not like the new so-called elven "monarch." What kind of leader sent his troops to prey on caravans—and what kind of troops obeyed that order? Mercenaries would, of course, but soldiers with a sworn loyalty?

The official trusted none of it.

He leaned back in his chair and chewed absentmindedly on one finger—no matter how old you got, you had bad habits—when something sizzled behind him.

The noise was instantly familiar. He turned in his chair and narrowed his eyes. Admittedly, he wasn't the world's most competent wizard when it came to quick spells, which had always made it difficult for him to excel in combat. He was, however, exceedingly methodical and very good at making his spells almost impenetrable.

Which meant that the person currently trying to cast a spell that would affect his personal quarters should have no luck.

The sizzle came again, then once more. Another attempt followed soon after and there was a long pause before the fifth.

Shouting erupted in the hall.

Jaco smiled thinly before he stood and wiped the tired grimace off his face. When the door opened for two guardsmen, he waited in his formal robes and smiled slightly.

"A visitor?" he asked.

"An elf, sir."

"A representative of King Yn'sur I!" an outraged voice called after them, and a very ostentatiously dressed elf pushed in behind the guards.

"One does not," he observed. "generally say, *the first* until a second king of the same name. Correct protocol is to use, *first of his name.*"

One of his favorite things to do, out of anything, was to use etiquette to annoy people. In this case, it worked wonders. The elf's face darkened in anger.

"King Yn'sur I has deigned to meet with you," he said angrily. "First, you deny entrance to a royal emissary and now you—a mere human servant—lecture me on manners?"

"Where I come from, emissaries don't appear in one's bedchamber in the dead of night," he said blandly. He twitched the scroll out of the elf's hand and scanned the words quickly. "Two days. He wants to meet in two *days?*"

The emissary raised his nose and sniffed. "King Yn'sur I has spoken." He swished one hand, clearly expecting to disappear in a puff of smoke. Instead, the sizzling noise came again.

Jaco's lips twitched as the elf marched out of the room to perform his transportation spell, but as soon as he was gone, he frowned. Who could he get to the rendezvous in two days?

And *what* did the letter mean about sending 'a true icon of strength?'

CHAPTER TWENTY-EIGHT

Dotty opened her eyes to see the plain brown interior of a tent. She turned her head slowly and felt fur beneath her cheek. Her whole body felt cushioned, soft, and warm. She let her eyes drift closed again with a happy sigh.

Then she remembered what had happened before she lost consciousness. Her eyes snapped open and she looked around for anyone else.

Lyle was reading in the corner of the tent. She watched him for a moment and saw the tension in the way he held the book. He ignored her little cot with utter determination. And were his eyes red from crying?

She gathered her resolve to sit and, to her surprise, was able to do so fairly easily. When she met his gaze, she smiled at him. "You know," she told him, "I had promised I wouldn't keel over."

He tried to smile in return but his chin trembled and he didn't manage to say anything. Instead, he put the book down carefully and looked at her for a long moment. "Ye were in pain. The shamans came an' did a spell over ye, and ye've slept better since. Most o' the day."

"I'm sorry," she whispered.

"No. I'm sorry." He closed his eyes for a moment. "I kept hopin' it wasn't real. I keep thinkin' o' the things I didn't say."

Dotty frowned at him. "What do you mean?" She was cold and she drew a soft, woven blanket around her.

"All the times when I joked instead o' tellin' you how well ye were doin' in trainin'," he said. He looked away from her. "I would never have been so hard on ye, back when we first met, if I'd known."

"Lyle—I didn't tell you." She shook her head. "And I felt much better then. I wasn't so tired. Although I feel well right now." Under her breath, she added: "Prima?"

"A doctor came. They gave you painkillers. It's brought the pain down to levels that you can't feel it in-game." The AI sounded upset. *"I tried, you know. But I couldn't do it."*

"Prima." Dotty shook her head helplessly. "There's only so much anyone can do."

She waited and although the AI said nothing more, she could practically feel her misery radiating.

Lyle, meanwhile, still struggled to regain his composure. He had nodded jerkily at her but he fixed his gaze on the ground.

"Lyle?" she asked.

"It's not only...ye," he said. "There's a lot o' people I didn't speak to as much as I should. Me father an' I never mended things afore he died." He sighed and looked up. "An' here ye are, dyin', an' I'm makin' all this about me."

Dotty smiled slightly.

The tent flap opened and a young orc entered. He held a big jug of steaming water and a fresh cloth, and behind him came another with a platter of food. Both nodded respectfully to Dotty and one said to Lyle, "The shamans have extended you an offer to dine with them if you wish, sir."

The dwarf looked at her.

She nodded. "Go. Some time to wash and eat will be appreciated. Tell them I am awake and I am well."

He gave her a wordless nod and left with the others.

Even though her stomach was rumbling, she decided to wash before eating. She stripped and began to wipe warm water over her skin. There was a bar of soap, rough and overwhelmingly scented with herbs, but it reminded her of growing up with her grandmother's homemade soap.

"I've received word from the researchers," Prima said finally.

"Hmm?" She realized that her mind had drifted. The painkillers they gave her must have been something.

"The doctor came, as you know, and gave you medication. There were scans as well, I believe. They've called your family to come to the lab, but there are several hours before everyone will be assembled."

Dotty put the washcloth down slowly. "It's close, then."

A pause followed. *"Yes and no. They don't know when, but your condition is not critical yet. The team asked me to tell you the following."*

"Oh?"

"As your condition is not critical, would you like them to arrange for one last mission before you come out of the game?" Prima tried to disguise it, but there was no missing the hope in her voice. *"They say that, in the doctor's opinion, there should be no danger. It is only a matter of if you feel well enough to do so."*

She thought about the offer in silence. Wind whistled over the mesa and she could hear children running and shrieking outside, along with sharp reminders from their parents to stay away from the cliffs. She slipped her dress over her shoulders and ducked out to watch the activity.

A few of the orcs noticed her and gave awkward nods, respectful and awed, but the rest were too engrossed in their celebrations and negotiations. She smiled as she watched. Fire tribe members demonstrated the workings of a forge, and a water tribe member instructed several others on the best way to weave fishing nets. Some tents had colorful blankets on the ground outside them, spread with beautiful wares.

No. She wasn't ready to leave yet, no matter the exhaustion that pulled at her bones.

"One more mission," she murmured. "Yes, Prima. I'd like that."

"I'll make sure there's some luxury to keep you amused," the AI assured her. On the one hand, it seemed ridiculous to read emotion into the flat, mechanical voice but on the other, she could not help but do so.

Dotty ate quickly but savored each mouthful of grilled meat and vegetables. She wrapped different assortments in flatbread and dolloped chutneys on with abandon.

One chutney, in particular, proved to be a mistake.

"Oh, God in heaven." She eyed her dagger and resisted the urge to slice her tongue off. "Prima, what did I just eat?"

"In your world, I'm told they're called ghost peppers."

"Oh, no." She lowered her face into her hands and remembered only at the last moment to not get her fingers anywhere near her eyes. "As my mother would say, Sweet Moses."

"The shamans would be available to see you if you wanted a distraction—as would Atra."

"I'm not sure I should see Atra," she said. She stood and stumbled out of the tent. "On the other hand, maybe—Atra." She stopped dead.

The woman was standing outside. She must have been waiting for her to come out and something seemed different about her. Cautiously, she scanned the warrior, taking in the necklace of polished beach stones and the copper ring in one tusk. Everything seemed the same, so she was left a little bewildered.

Oh. No weapon.

Dotty exhaled slow. "You should know—" she said.

At the same time, Atra said, "I came to say—"

Both of them broke off, and the younger woman gestured at her.

"You should know that your words changed the negotiations

for the better," she said. "We won't interfere. Our mages and historians will come to help yours uncover what the dragons tried to destroy of your past. That and an ambassador, nothing more."

Atra stared at her.

"And, for what it is worth—although it may not be enough—I apologize." She shook her head. "I ask only that you think more kindly of me. Before I met you, I stood between the tribe at Mountain's Shadow and a dragon who taunted me with the fact that it had lied to them. There was no time to make a more… nuanced…choice."

The warrior looked away. Her hands were clenched into fists. "I know." The two words were grudging and she clearly did not want to say them.

Dotty smiled slightly. Such was the experience of youth—so much raw pride tumbling in one's chest. Atra had not yet grown used to such things.

Indeed, the young woman looked at her as if she was gathering courage to say something. She took a few deep breaths, and finally said, "I'm still angry."

"I know," she told her simply. "And perhaps you always will be."

Atra frowned.

"Your tribe is in good hands," she said. "I have watched how much you and the other young ones love them and how much strength they bring to the prospect of rebuilding. Atra, in sixty years, when you are my age and you watch the young ones, remember to trust *them* as well." She went to walk away toward the main tent but stopped. "And be well," she added.

It was not enough, but no words ever would be. Atra blinked, her eyes suspiciously bright.

"You, also," she said. She cleared her throat. "I hear…you may be ill."

"I am." Dotty smiled sadly at her. "But death comes to all of us.

A quiet death after a long life is not such a bad thing. Remember that too lest you ever be tempted to give your life for glory and battle." She reached out hesitantly to touch the other woman's cheek and then walked away.

When she entered the main tent, she stopped in shock.

"Hello," Jaco said.

"How are you here?" she asked him and looked at the others.

"I'm not precisely here." He walked forward through the fire. "See?"

"That looks somewhat apocalyptic—could you...not?" She ushered him out of the fire and sat in the chair an orc brought for her. "Have they spoken to you of the terms we agreed upon? There are some details to work out—if they agree to it, of course—"

"We voted to accept," Rashat rumbled.

"We are glad to share knowledge with the orcs," Jaco said, his demeanor dignified. He seemed far happier about this deal than the previous one. "I know several historians who have made it their life's work to study the orcs. I sent them word to copy any manuscripts they might have and prepare for a journey."

"I sent word to Berghold as well," Lyle said. "A few of the *zauberers* have volunteered already, or so I'm told."

"There will be the matter of choosing the ambassador," Jaco said to Dotty, "but I believe I can handle such negotiations. You are needed urgently elsewhere right now...if you can be spared."

She looked around her. Lyle nodded, as did Rashat. A few other chieftains were in the room—far from the full complement —but each of them nodded as well.

"I...certainly." She shrugged. "What is this new urgent need?"

Jaco looked briefly at the orcish leaders before he said casually, "Negotiations with the elven monarch."

Lyle swore and her eyes widened.

"I thought you came on behalf of Insea," Rashat said and frowned.

"Oh, we did." She sighed. "There's a faction of elves who have established a new monarchy—and made attacks on both Berghold and Insea. It would seem they have now agreed to a meeting." What a last mission. She wanted to laugh. "They introduced themselves blade-first the last time I met them, so we'll see what happens this time."

"Mmm." Jaco looked faintly evasive. "I'll brief you en route. I have developed a working that can have you and Lyle at the meeting site in a few hours."

"What?" Her eyes were wide. *How?*

He glared at her, a little offended. "I'll have you know that I was trained by the finest wizards in the world." He shrugged and added under his breath, "And I have access to a rather extensive collection of artifacts."

"Ah."

"The others will join you as well," he said. "Zaara says that *none* of you are to mention Kural's skin."

"His skin?"

"That is all I was told." He shrugged. "But…someone should find a way to send me an image."

Dotty gave him a thumbs-up. "We'll go pack and prepare, then."

He nodded and his image disappeared like smoke.

"Insea seeks peace with many," Rashat said. "And unless I miss my guess, this will be a particularly difficult negotiation."

"You have no idea," she said and rolled her eyes. "Elves are stuck-up bastards."

The orcs laughed, and the shaman came to clasp her hand. "I think this will be our final goodbye," he said. "Know that you will be remembered as a woman who sacrificed herself to defeat the false gods and who rallied us to fight together."

Her eyes brimmed with tears. "You could have given me no better words of farewell. Goodbye, friend."

CHAPTER TWENTY-NINE

Dotty wasn't sure what she had expected from the transportation spell, but it was most certainly nowhere close to reality.

After hurrying down the path at the edge of the mesa, she and Lyle were met by Jaco again, his form almost solid. He guided them on where to stand, made sure their ponies and the palanquin were within very stable parameters, and stepped back and promptly disappeared.

The two companions looked at one another.

"What do you think—" she began before they were enveloped in something that looked like a cloud.

The ground—although she could feel it under her feet—was invisible and the clouds around them began to whirl. She stood still next to one of the ponies and stroked her nose, shushing and murmuring comforting things. Lyle did the same and both of them waited for the jolt of movement.

After an embarrassingly long pause, she looked up and around. "Prima?"

Her companion glanced at her, confused, and she shook her head at him.

"Mm-hmm?" Prima asked. The AI sounded like she wanted to laugh.

"Are we moving?" she asked severely.

"Yes. Yes, you are."

"Is there any way to tell where we are?" she asked.

She should have known better, she realized a split-second later, but it was too late. The clouds around them vanished and she was able to see the landscape racing far below them. It was somewhat like being in a plane but without any of the visual barriers that—she now realized—made plane travel possible for humans.

Lyle yelled a protest. The ponies seemed to not notice at all.

"Prima," Dotty said and tried to maintain a calm tone, "put the cloud back."

The barrier appeared and the AI said in faux innocence, *"But you wanted to see."*

"You knew," she accused. "You knew it would scare the crap out of us and you—oh! Justin! Hi!"

Indeed, their little haven from the outside air had suddenly broadened as if two bubbles had merged, and Justin and Tina were now visible.

"Dotty!" The young woman ran to her. She wore her leather armor and would have looked exceedingly threatening if she wasn't crying.

"Tina." She wrapped her arms around her. "Are you safe? Are you well?"

"Me?" Tina looked incredulously at her. "We got word from Prima. About…you."

"Ah." She looked at the cloud. "Prima, could we have somewhere to sit?"

The cloud obligingly formed itself into a few benches and Justin ambled closer to sit with a very-confused looking Lyle as Dotty and Tina sat together.

"Tell me about your adventures," she said gently and squeezed the young woman's hand. "I hear there were some very close calls with nobility who were determined to make marriage deals."

"Oh, you wouldn't *believe*." The woman rolled her eyes. Diverted, she launched into a story that involved no less than five suitors, a series of increasingly transparent ruses, and—to her surprise—a trained giraffe. Even Lyle and Justin came to hear the story, and the young man interjected with occasional anecdotes. The dwarf guffawed at some of the stranger tactics the human nobility had used.

Tina was mimicking the giraffe with one arm when the bubble burst again, this time to reveal Zaara and Kural, and everyone stopped talking at once.

The wizard was blue. It was a very nice shade of blue, but human skin was not meant to be that color. It wasn't paint, either, and Dotty hoped for his sake that it wasn't a tattoo.

Everyone stared at him, he stared back, and behind him, Zaara made furious gestures to not talk about it.

Dotty cleared her throat. "Everyone's here! Good. We should probably discuss our plan with the elves."

"Awww," Tina muttered.

Kural stalked to the group and sat on one of the cloud benches.

"He's a little upset right now," Zaara said in a stage whisper, "because this is a very complex working and he didn't get to do it."

"Oh, is that why?" Justin asked blandly.

Zaara gave him a glare that would have turned him to stone if she had the ability.

Lyle, meanwhile, had retrieved his ale mug and desperately tried to hide his laughter behind it. All Dotty could see was his shoulders shaking with silent mirth and the top of his head.

"So," she said, trying to hide her amusement, "what do we know about the elven offer of peace talks?"

Kural withdrew a scroll from one sleeve and unrolled it. He

cleared his throat, the very picture of offended dignity, and began to read. The offer, although incredibly wordy, had very little actual content to it—quite simply, it invited the representatives of Insea to a neutral meeting ground.

"They couldn't simply have said *yes?*" Tina asked when he had finished. "Yes, we'll talk to you?"

"You haven't met any elves, have you?" Zaara asked her. "Wordy fuckers, the lot of 'em."

Before anyone else could speak, the cloud suddenly vanished and was replaced by gently rolling grassland with pink grass and tall, ethereal flowers that almost seemed to float. A quarter of a mile away, an elven camp with an impossibly complex tent that looked like a castle drew their attention. Guards marched in formation around the fake castle and, on the ground outside it, stood a dais with a throne. The figure seated there shone as brightly as the sun, from his gold-crowned head to his gold-armored body.

"I wonder which one is the king," Lyle said.

"It could be any of them," Tina said, her expression deadpan. "They all have *very* fancy hats."

Kural looked at them. "You two, behave. We've been seen."

Indeed, a shout had gone up and a detachment of mounted soldiers galloped across the plain to surround the party.

"Identify yourselves," one of them said crisply.

"We are the emissaries from Insea," Kural responded. He held the scroll up with the elven king's seal.

The soldiers nodded stiffly. No apology was made for their overly armed greeting, and they marched the group to the tent without any further words. One soldier swung down from his horse and knelt before the king before he rose to whisper in his ear.

The monarch's gaze swept over them. His eyes were a startling and vivid shade of purple and his skin held a blue tinge. He was not old, Dotty guessed—at least, his hair was not gray and his skin looked smooth—but she had no idea what older elves looked like.

And, under all that armor, he might have any physique.

"You are the emissaries sent from Insea?" he asked them. The corner of his mouth twitched slightly.

"Yes, your grace." She had, somewhere in the midst of the journey, been garbed in another golden confection of a gown, this one held up with citrines.

Her disapproving gaze noted the way the king looked at Lyle with his serviceable gear, Tina, Justin, and Zaara in their armor, and Kural with his strange, blue skin. He respected her, although only tenuously. The rest of them, he respected not at all.

"The representatives of Insea have arrived," he said. His voice carried magically across the space. "We await this outcome with interest. Prepare your strength." He raised a hand, bored, and shooed them away.

"Wait, what?" She stepped forward, but the group was immediately surrounded by soldiers who ushered them to a plaza on the side of the makeshift courtyard. They left, although two of them took position a few yards away.

Dotty looked at the others. "What on earth is going on?"

"He awaits the outcome," Kural muttered. "Strength...they keep saying strength...what does that mean?"

When the whole picture fell into place, Dotty groaned.

"What?" he asked quietly. "What is it?"

"I get it," she said. She shook her head wearily. "It's a trial by combat."

"What? But that's—"

"Barbaric?" she suggested. "A stupid way to test one's ability to rule? Yes. But that appears to be their custom and that's what they want from us." She pressed her hand softly against her stomach and wished that her body wasn't hurting quite so much. "Lyle could do it, maybe."

The others had drifted closer. When Kural briefed them with a single, terse sentence, their eyes widened.

"We should tell Jaco what's going on," Justin said finally.

"No." The wizard spread the scroll. "We've agreed not to. See here? I thought this phrase meant absolutely nothing—*the representatives being chosen as the representatives*—but it's hiding elven law behind the tautology. When Jaco sent us and we arrived, everyone here became locked into the negotiations. They can't call in anyone or communicate with anyone outside this campground, and neither can we."

"So they tricked us," Dotty said. "Son of a—"

"So we've agreed to handle it the way they say," Justin said as he worked through the problem. "We've agreed one of *us* will be the one to handle it...and it has to be a trial by combat." He looked at Kural, who nodded. "Great. That's great."

"It's not bad," Lyle said.

Everyone gave him an incredulous look.

"What?" He shrugged. "I've watched every one o' you face monsters an' all kinds o' fights. We simply have to choose which one of us is doin' this. I don' think we can make a wrong choice, to be honest."

A pause dragged on while they considered what he'd said.

"He has a point," Zaara stated.

"I say Zaara or Justin," Tina said. "Both of them have magic and weapons skills."

The other woman looked uncomfortable. "Having peace with the elven monarchy riding on me?"

"You said it was a good idea," the dwarf reminded her.

"I meant in general! Not...*me*." She shuddered. "What if I slip? What if my dagger gets caught in the sheath? All of a sudden, outright war because of a leg cramp or something. Too much pressure."

"Someone has to do it," Dotty pointed out. "And Tina's right. You two are the logical choices."

Justin looked faintly green. "But she makes a good point. And I've fucked up so much in this world."

"Yes," Prima said drily, *"you have."*

"Hey!"

"No dithering," she said firmly. "We'll toss a coin. Both of you are good choices."

"Or…" Lyle said speculatively. He shook his head. "Nah."

"Spit it out, Lyle."

"Well, there's one other person here who has both magic and weapons skills." He pointed at her. "I didn't say it at first because ye're not feeling so great, but it might be a good choice. You aren't quite so easily rattled as these two."

Both Zaara and Justin looked like they would very much like to protest but accepted the judgment with mutters instead.

"Me?" she said blankly. "I can't do it!"

"Why not?" he asked.

"I'm not—you need someone in better shape who has been properly trained with weapons, not an old woman who only started with them a few months back!"

"Ye're forgettin' ye've *already* fought one o' their champions— and won." He gave her a hard look. "Remember that warrior in the black armor? An' I've seen ye on the road. Ye're sneaky *an'* ye're brave."

"Ohhh." Dotty sat on the bench with a thump. "Oh, I don't know that I should do this."

She looked at where the king conversed with his top aides. Every one of them flashed their armor and weapons ostenta- tiously and laughed behind their hands at Insea's delegation. She'd seen enough of those people in real life, the type who had never faced any consequences and liked to bully others because they thought they were untouchable. So many times, she had counseled her children to ignore them, do their work, and focus on their results.

Maybe she had chosen the wrong path all those times. The thought made her frown.

And maybe she had a chance to show this world there were other options sometimes.

Dotty looked up and winked at Justin and Tina.

The woman bounced and clapped. "You'll do it!"

"Yeah, I think I will." She stood. "I might as well go out on a high note, and if I'm *honest*...punching that guy in the face would most certainly be a high note."

CHAPTER THIRTY

Dotty was given a tent in which to change into her armor. Despite the urgent whispers from the others, she sent them away and started to pace. She had a few minutes before anyone would come to call her.

"You'll want to project a somewhat more intimidating effect when you get outside," Prima told her.

"Uh-huh." She watched as some kind of pre-armor gear appeared on her arms and legs. It was bronze, close-fitting, and oddly heavy. She wasn't a fan of heaviness for its own sake but right now, it seemed comforting and safe.

The gauntlets she'd worn in Insea appeared again, the daggers sheathed inside them, and her hair was pulled back more tightly and the jeweled pins were removed. She frowned and waited for the rest.

"Prima?"

"Yes?"

"Where's my armor?"

"That is your armor."

"This?" Dotty looked up incredulously. "It's…spandex."

"It's not spandex," the AI protested as if she were rolling her eyes. *"Try stabbing yourself."*

"I'd much rather not."

"Just try it, you baby."

Dotty glared, drew one of the daggers, and aimed toward her stomach. After a moment's thought, she decided to try to pull the hem of her pants away from her leg and stab that instead. To her surprise, the slight motion sent shockwaves rippling up her arm and hardly seemed to dent the fabric.

She tried again, harder this time, with the same result. Her third attempt was a hard strike to her stomach, and the exclamation that resulted was from the pain in her arms, not where the blade had landed.

"This is extraordinary." She remembered the plate armor outside. "But…isn't it cheating?"

"No."

"Prima, I'm serious."

"So am I," the AI said. *"This type of armor was made by the elves originally. Everyone knows about it but it's expensive to produce. The people out there have access to it if they want it but they don't think it looks impressive enough."*

"Oh, so they're being stupid?"

"Yes."

"Then I'm fine with it." Dotty nodded. "I'm ready to go."

She pushed out of the tent and was escorted onto the plaza. A magical barrier sprang into place around a circle of ground and denoted where the fight would take place. The sound around her had lowered drastically.

No one would be able to call recommendations to her. The thought made her swallow uncomfortably.

On the other hand, no one would be able to heckle her, either.

All thoughts vanished when her opponent stepped into the ring. He wore plate armor like the king and he had more human coloring—blond hair and green eyes. When he moved, it was as if the massively-heavy armor was no impediment. From the ease with which he drew his broadsword, she assumed he had trained as a warrior from the time he could walk.

He gave her a look that said he would enjoy cutting her in half. "Barbarian."

Dotty raised an eyebrow. She had never been very good with quick comebacks and now that she had missed her moment to give him one, they flooded to her mind.

"The rules of every civilized duel apply," the king said simply. His voice traveled into the circle without hindrance, and she could see the smirk on his face. He dared her to ask what those were and admit she wasn't civilized.

"What do elves consider civilized?" she asked.

It wasn't *quite* a disrespectful question. She kept a pleasant smile on her face as the king's smile grew slightly more strained.

"Magic will protect contestants from death," he said, "but not from permanent injury. The results will be binding, and the barrier will protect any wind or other outside force from disrupting the proceedings. The match is concluded when one opponent yields, is injured enough to invoke the magical protections, or stays on the ground for a count of ten."

"Elves *are* civilized," she said. She let the implied "who would have guessed" hang in the air and studied her opponent.

He looked like he wanted to murder her, but she could handle that. Honestly, he wouldn't be the first.

Harry's first girlfriend, for instance, hadn't been too fond of her.

The barrier flared and went opaque and the elven warrior charged without warning.

Dotty dodged sideways and darted under his raised arms as he brought the broadsword down. The ground shuddered under her feet and she whirled to see that he had gouged a deep cut into the packed dirt. He wrenched the sword free and looked at her from under a drifting tendril of blond hair, and her heart seized.

This was the kind of person Tina and Justin had spoken of. This was the type who tried to kill in the arena, who would do his damnedest to strike a killing blow before the magic could save her.

And if that death would save something she loved, she would consider it. But if he won, he would gain an advantage in the negotiations and she would be *damned* if she let that happen.

She let her eyes drift closed for a split-second before she refocused as they began to circle. In her mind, she pictured the haze of dust above a South Carolina road on a hot day and the way it stung the eyes and itched in the throat.

The warrior blinked a few times and tossed his head. One hand came away from the sword to wave at the air around him, and she pictured the billow of dust rising behind a battered old truck. The air around his head turned golden brown, filled with a haze of dust that drifted into his eyes and his nose. He frowned, she smiled, and his face turned murderous.

"Heathen magic," he hissed.

"Oh, you have *no* idea," she told him. "I've studied with orcs, I've studied with dwarves—honestly, every kind of heathen you can imagine."

He opened his mouth to speak and the dust rushed in so instead, he spat and coughed. "Bitch."

"Yep," she agreed and nodded.

He yelled and attacked and again, she dodged. Twice, she spun away and once passed only inches below a single-handed swing of the broadsword. She frowned as its shadow whistled above her.

Goddamn, this elf was strong. Was that natural?

The question was irrelevant, she supposed, given that they were already in combat.

"Fight me like a warrior!" he called furiously. "Not like a witch."

"I'm sorry," Dotty said in amusement. She ducked another

swing and managed to land an elbow strike to the back of his head as he spun past. "Did you think you would taunt me into going one-on-one with swords merely by calling me a coward?"

"If you had any honor…" he began and she tuned out. She had heard this whole speech before—or whatever version of it boys did at her high school. He yelled obscenities and insults that were probably very grave, while she began to sense the flow in his movements and both the shocking speed and the relatively slow swings of the broadsword.

They might be slow, she realized, but they were also damned near unstoppable. She could *not* get in the way of those. The armor might stop an assassin's shiv but she was fairly sure it wouldn't do jack when hit by a train.

Finally, his face split into a savage, bitter smile. "*Fine,*" he snarled. "If that's how you're going to be." He ripped a pouch at his waist open and threw something at her.

His aim was precise, and the projectile struck with the force of a baseball—nor was there anywhere to run. It stung as it shattered against her skin and powder erupted to choke her with its fumes.

What the hell *was* it?

Dotty had no time to ponder it. She threw herself to one side, not even sure why she did it until her mind processed the sound of footsteps on gravel. He had shifted his weight to attack and only instinct had saved her.

She rolled onto her feet, ready to throw a jet of volcanic heat at his head and end this, but nothing came. Her magic bar was gray and a circle counted down next to it.

"Son of a bitch," she snapped. "He took my magic?"

"*Looks like,*" Prima said drily.

Dotty watched the circle count down to estimate how much time she had when the AI yelled a warning and she barely managed to evade a swing. He followed his weapon and drove her against the back wall. His plate mail crushed her chest and face as he snarled at her.

She slammed one knee upward and got only a grimace for her efforts—of *course* he was wearing a cup—before she tried to jab her fingers into two gaps in his armor. Hitting his neck only made his chin come down and slam the visor onto one hand, but her jab at his eyes made him stumble back with a yell.

Finally, she threw a leg up and shoved his retreating form with all her might.

He sprawled a little distance away, thank God, but he was up in the next moment with murder in his eyes and she still had no magic. When he attacked her this time, there was no hesitation. However he had trained, he could still swing this weapon quickly without tiring.

For now, she cleared every thought from her mind and devoted every ounce of energy to darting away from his attacks. There were too many near-misses to count as even without the weight of plate mail and a sword, she could not move much faster than he could. Worse, she was reacting.

She wasn't driving the fight, which put him firmly in control.

And how long could she hold out? Already, she had begun to tire. That brief moment of despair almost cost her an arm but she managed to swerve and twisted under his blade. Pain radiated from the glancing blow.

Instinct told her she needed to turn the tide, but how? Her mind racing, she dodged another strike. He was smiling triumphantly and knew he had the strength and stamina to outlast her.

In the upper part of her screen, the magic bar turned blue again. She uttered a yell of satisfaction and poured her power out into his armor. He screamed as the metal flared red-hot and he recoiled from her to strip pieces of it off and throw them aside.

Dotty almost wished she hadn't done that, because as soon as the armor was gone, she could see how muscly he was. It wasn't a picture that gave her a great deal of hope for the rest of the fight. He whirled with a curse on his lips but it died when he didn't see her.

Desperation had lent her innovation and she hurtled toward him at knee-level. She drove her shoulders into his knees and pushed off with all the strength in her legs to carry him over. He landed heavily with her on top and she fought the urge to pin him down and start punching him in the face. She *wanted* to do it but she had enough sense to realize that this gigantic warrior was, without a doubt, better at grappling than she was.

Instead, she rolled away with a jab of one elbow onto his shin. He howled in pain and stood shakily to limp on his injured leg.

"Barbarians," he declared belligerently, "should not have been allowed to *speak* to our king, let alone make demands of him!"

Dotty rolled her eyes and turned the ground under his feet white-hot. He yelped and danced away. His sword, unfortunately, was somehow immune to magic—or was made of a metal that didn't respond in the same way toward heat. She circled as she considered what else could she do—something that wouldn't kill him but *would* hurt him enough to disable him and gain the victory.

The answer came to her as she surged forward and she threw her hands out, her palms facing him.

Magic pounded into him like a wall. It had the force of a wave to lift and circle, the heat of a volcano, and the crushing pressure that lay below the earth. This was the earth magic she had first learned from dwarven manuscripts, the power of fire that Huwat had shown her, and the deathly cold force of the deep ocean Rashat had summoned against the dragons.

And along with it, the surprise factor learned from a certain dwarf named Stout.

Hot and cold, force and fire, caught the elf full in the face and he went over on his back. She dropped to her knees and dragged air into her chest with desperate breaths. With him down—and a count being shouted by the whole crowd—she had time to feel the burning in her lungs and the ache in her muscles.

And the sharp pain in her stomach and the taste of metal in her mouth.

She pulled herself up, more because she wanted to lie down than because she wanted to look triumphant, but she stood until the count reached ten and she raised one arm in a motion of victory. The wall disappeared around her and her first sight was the *very* welcome expression of panic on the king's face. She grinned at him even as she swayed.

"Are you okay?" Prima asked urgently.

"I need to…get away. To sit." She muttered the words under her breath.

An elven servant appeared with a folding chair a moment later and lowered his head. He was either very good at hiding his feelings or he didn't mind much that the king and his champion had suffered a setback.

They probably weren't very nice to servants, she thought vaguely. She should tell the others that they could get good information that way.

"Dotty?" Tina chafed her hands. "Are you—is it—"

"Time to go home," Dotty said. The taste of metal was stronger but she smiled at them. Her head was spinning slightly. "You have all been the best traveling companions I could wish for. What adventures we've had."

"Dotty." Prima's voice was urgent. *"Before you go—"*

"This isn't goodbye," she murmured. Tina was crying silently. Justin stood with his arm around her and Lyle held one of her hands. "Not for the two of us, Prima."

She almost *felt* her nod. Then, the AI said, *"I'll tell them you're ready to wake up."*

CHAPTER THIRTY-ONE

It wasn't a bad place for a goodbye, Dotty thought dreamily. The pale cloth of the tent fluttered at the edges with glimpses of the fairytale landscape beyond.

Kural hung back at the door, making sure that no self-important elves interrupted the proceeding. At his side, Zaara hovered awkwardly. Tina was crying quietly. Justin's arm was around her and his cheeks were wet with tears. Lyle knelt beside the cot, one hand wrapped around hers.

Tina said her goodbye first. She wiped her eyes, knelt at the bed, and laced her hands through hers as she smiled at her through the tears.

"I never thought I'd get to do shots with a grandmother," she said finally. Her voice cracked, but when Dotty laughed, she did as well. "Dotty, I lost my abuela when I was seven. She was so strict, but my mom had stories from her father—she said my abuela used to be wild. She ran the family ranch for a few years when she was young and was a crack shot. I never believed it because she was so keen to have me be ladylike."

She paused for a moment, looked down, and tried to swallow her tears.

"Seeing you, hearing you joke, watching you take no shit—I feel closer to her than I ever did while she was alive. I used to be so scared of getting older. I thought the best of my life would have passed me by. And I'm not scared anymore. Thank you."

Dotty smiled as she cupped the woman's cheek in her hand. "You'll be so much more than any one person ever knows," she promised her. "You'll change lives and worlds. And when you're older and your grandchildren think you're simply a quiet old woman, you'll know better. You'll have learned to make a hell of a fuss so it creates the most impact."

Tina nodded and leaned over to kiss her cheek. She stood and Justin took her place.

"I never know what to say at times like this," he admitted.

"Words aren't the only way to show someone you care," she said and squeezed his hand.

"No, I want to try." He swallowed. "I've changed so much in this game, but I always felt like it was my place in a way. I was the first one here. I was raised on video games. When you got here, I thought I'd be the one to show you the ropes—and you'd already outstripped me in some ways." He swallowed. "I don't think I know yet how much I've learned from you. I wish I did so I could tell you."

A tear trickled down the side of her face. "Some things aren't ours to know," she told him quietly. "You be good, young man. Be someone who makes you proud of yourself."

He nodded before he kissed her cheek and moved back so Lyle could shuffle closer.

"I…" The dwarf swallowed and looked away. "I can't."

"I'll speak," Zaara said and stepped alongside him. She kissed Lyle on the cheek. "You think of your words."

Dotty smiled.

Zaara smoothed her hair back from her head. She hesitated for a moment, then pulled one of her daggers out. "My…in my village, a warrior is buried holding a weapon. I would be honored if you were to accept this blade from me. I was honored to fight alongside you."

She nodded, her throat so tight she couldn't speak.

The woman folded Dotty's hands around the hilt and rested them on her chest. Her chin began to tremble. "I'm—ah…I'm never going to have children of my own," she forced herself to say. "Wizards—don't, you know. But my brother will, my friends will, and I'll watch all of them grow old and have children of their own. I'll watch generations of them be born and die, and what you've done here—it'll give them all peace. Thank you."

Dotty met her gaze and nodded. Zaara moved to join the huddle with Tina and Justin, both of whom wrapped their arms around her.

"Ah." Lyle cleared his throat. "I'm like Justin, with not much of a way with words."

"You know that's not true." She smiled at him. "You taught me to fight, Lyle Stout. You think you're a mercenary with no finer sentiments, but that's far from true. I've never seen a man more devoted to his people."

"I left them," he said bluntly.

"You did," she agreed, "in order to learn what you needed to know. We can't always fix the places we love with only what we already know."

His fingers tightened around hers. "I've been honored to know ye," he said hoarsely.

"And I you," she whispered. Her head was spinning. She squeezed his fingers once more and looked over his head at Kural.

He knew what her look meant. "I'll keep them safe," he promised her.

Dotty nodded her thanks. She closed her eyes for a moment and focused on the feel of Lyle's hands around hers.

The world began to dissolve at the edges, and the next time she opened her eyes, it was in the all-white of the laboratory and the faces she saw, the fingers wrapped around hers, belonged to her children.

"You're here," she said quietly.

They nodded. Mary was crying. Ellen's eyes were dry but their depths brimmed with pain.

"I'm glad you're here," she said.

"We're *all* here," John said. His voice was tight and he leaned away before he came back into view with Liam in his arms. "Even the very little ones."

"Oh." Dotty picked her hand up and brushed it across the boy's hair. "It is so good to see you, little one."

The child knew something was wrong. He clung to his grandfather and began to cry.

"It's okay," she told him. "It's okay, Liam."

Mary turned away with her shoulders shaking. Her hands were pressed over her face.

"Sometimes, we have to say…goodbye." It hurt. It hurt so much right now but she forced a smile. Dimly, she felt someone take her arm and an IV port jostled. Her hand felt cool a moment later, and the comfort spread outward.

She stretched her hand toward Liam and a moment later, he moved his tiny hand to meet hers.

"Goodbyes are sad," she told him. "Mmm?"

He stared at her, his little blue eyes confused.

"But there's nothing to be afraid of," she told him. "You be good, Liam. You be strong. There's nothing to be afraid of."

She kissed his head before his parents came to take him from John's arms. They kissed her forehead and whispered goodbyes. One by one, the littlest children came to hug her and their parents handed them off so that they could say goodbye as well.

"I'm so lucky to get to say goodbye to all of you," Dotty said. She saw them draw closer, the fractures and spats between them gone for the moment—dark hair and fair, the glimmers of Harry's smile, and the golden-brown highlights of her hair. For a moment, she thought she could see their futures spinning out from this moment—their choices, their loves, their moments of triumph and grief, their achievements, and their lazy days on the porch and into their old age.

They would be okay.

Everyone else drew back for the children to say goodbye to Dotty. She smiled at them.

"I am so proud of you," she said. "Every one of you."

Robert looked uncertain. Her bachelor child. Dotty beckoned him close for a kiss on the forehead. "I'm proud of you," she whispered. "So was your father. We love you."

"I love you, too." He kissed her on the forehead as well. "I love you, Mom."

Deborah was next, smoothing her hair as they whispered their goodbyes. She was keeping it together for now. She would, her mother knew, and she would fall apart later in private. She met Todd's eyes over Deborah's head. *Look after her,* the look said. He nodded and put a hand silently over his heart. She smiled at him.

Ellen was crying when she came to hold her hand. She leaned close and put her forehead against hers. "Being inside the game with you will be one of my best memories," she said quietly. "Who you were there…" She trailed off.

She didn't need to finish the sentence. Dotty nodded. "I'm sorry," she said again. It wasn't enough. No words would change the past. But she and Ellen, at least in this moment, were at peace with that.

John and Mary went last. This was the first time Dotty had seen her daughter-in-law disheveled and tear-streaked. She smiled at the two of them.

"Thank you for the cake," she said finally.

Mary laughed and finished with a little sob. She nodded.

"Don't spend too much time grieving," she told them. "Hmm?"

"I'm a grown man," John said, "and I'll grieve as long as I want, thank you." He cracked a smile, although his eyes were bright, and squeezed her hand when she laughed. "I'll miss you, Mom."

"And I'll miss you. I love you."

"I love you," John whispered. The others echoed it. "Do you want us to stay with you, Mom?"

"I'd like that," she said. "And one other thing. If I could."

They nodded.

"I'd like to…go back into the game," she said.

The children nodded.

"They said you might want that," John managed to say calmly. "They can put you in and keep the top open."

Dotty nodded. Dr. DuBois moved to her side and gave her a smile and a quiet nod as he pressed a few buttons. The IV port jostled again slightly.

Her children held her hand, all their hands piled one on top of the other, while the virtual reality took hold once more and her vision faded to the deep blue of twilight.

This wasn't a place she recognized. She walked through the interior of what looked like a cathedral, its vaulted ceiling high above and her path flanked by verdant trees that rustled with an invisible wind. Dawn light flooded through the tall windows. The air was warm and heavy with greenery, a summer morning. Her feet were bare on the stone floor.

"Prima?"

"*Yes?*"

"This is beautiful." She looked around and smiled in awe. "Thank you. Thank you, thank you, thank you."

A long pause was disturbed only by birds singing somewhere. "*Thank you,*" Prima said.

"We had good adventures, didn't we?"

"*Very good. You surprised me quite a few times.*" After a moment, she added, "*That was a compliment.*"

"I know." Dotty smiled. She reached the end of the cathedral, where wide double doors opened into a plain of waving grass. A mountain in the distance called to mind her time with the orcs. The sky was pale golds and blues. "I'm…not sure how far I can walk, Prima." For the first time, her heart seized. "I'm scared."

She knew what the AI wanted to say—that she was as well. But what she said instead, was, *"I'm here."*

"I'm glad." Tears trickled down her cheeks at last. "To have another morning like this, to see the sky—it's a gift I could never have imagined." She gulped a sob. "I don't know what's coming."

"You didn't know what was coming when you first got here," Prima said gently, *"and look how well you did with that."*

In an eyeblink, she was pillowed on a soft bed. It felt like she was in a hammock on a lazy summer day or a boat drifting on a pond. She elevated above the plain as the sun began to rise.

This time, instead of shielding her eyes, she didn't look away from the sun. The gold, the beauty filtering through the sky, and the warmth on her skin told her she was home.

"Don't be sad," Dotty said. It was close now.

"There's no need to fear sadness," Prima said gently. Quietly, she added, *"I do, though. You gave me a name. You called me to life, Dotty. And I promise you this—you will live on with me."*

The sun's warmth seeped all through her now. The birdsong had changed somehow. She felt it deep in her bones—or perhaps her edges had dissolved—and she was everywhere. Peace settled with the certainty that she *was* the morning and the sunshine and the birdsong.

Dotty closed her eyes.

EPILOGUE

Wind rustled in the trees as Ellen knelt at the graveside. She brushed her hand over the inscription in the stone and smiled at the scent of the peonies around the grave. Her mother had always loved peonies, had enjoyed the decadence of them and their blooms so rich and full.

"I miss you," she said quietly. "All of you—everything I knew and everything I didn't."

She stood and stared at the sky. Far in the distance, on one side of the plain, rain was falling. Lightning flickered in the clouds above. The sky on the other side of the plain was clear and sunlit and grass rippled.

"She is not gone." The voice made her jump. *"She is still here."*

Bemused, she scanned her surroundings. "She is?"

"Always." A woman's image flickered in front of her, young and carefree, spinning magic from her fingertips, wielding daggers, bowing in a throne room, and facing a dragon.

Ellen smiled through the tears.

"I don't know what to do," she whispered. The tears came more freely now. She sat in the grass and let the grief pour out of her. "I don't know what to do. This hurts so much."

The AI said nothing, but she felt it waiting there like a friend. It said nothing while the tears trickled into hiccups and she wiped her face. It made a bowl of cool water and a soft cloth appear beside her, for which she murmured a quiet thanks while she cleaned her face.

And then, when she was done crying and she settled her arms around her knees and gazed at the plains, it said quietly,

"Do you want your own adventures?"

Nick put a mug of tea in front of Simon.

"Thanks." The man's lanky frame was folded awkwardly into one of the chairs. "How long?"

"They're still getting all the monitors in place," he said comfortingly. "Everything is being monitored. They'll start tracking the feedback from the patches next." He smiled. "Her doctor and DuBois are becoming best buddies. I don't understand half the words they're using, but they seem very excited by some of the feedback they've seen so far."

Simon nodded. Beside him, Aimee curled on the couch with Emilia's head pillowed on her shoulder. Jamie had curled the other way, but his hand and Emilia's were linked. It had been two hours since Taigan had arrived at the Diatek headquarters, and it was approaching three AM.

Nick sat to wait. The father's eyes had not wavered from the pod even once.

And then, as they watched, the doctors closed the lid over Taigan and the monitors flickered on.

Blue. She hadn't seen anything in so long and now, there was *blue* and it was the most beautiful thing she'd ever seen. Taigan whirled and released an incredulous laugh. She had been trapped, she'd been—

Where was she?

She looked down and her body was only vaguely there.

Did she exist? She tried to take another step and sprawled awkwardly. Sitting was difficult, but she managed it. This place was blue and stars and nothing else. She didn't know where she was and fear began to creep in.

But she existed. She comforted herself with that. If she could think, she *existed*—wherever she was.

"Hello."

A young woman stood a short distance away, only a few years older than herself. Her hair was drawn back in a crown of braids. She wore a gown that made Taigan's jaw drop—silk of a green so dark that it was almost black held up at the arms by tiny opals. She held her hand out.

When she merely stared in response, the woman heaved an exasperated sigh. "Will you spend all day there?" she asked.

"Uh…no." She took the proffered hand and allowed herself to be pulled up. "Sorry. Thank you. Who are you?"

"I'm Dotty," the woman said. "And you are?"

The story continues with *One Broken Life*, book Seven in the P.I.V.O.T. Lab Chronicles.

Coming soon to Amazon and to Kindle Unlimited

CONNECT WITH MICHAEL ANDERLE

Website: http://lmbpn.com

Email List: http://lmbpn.com/email/

Social Media:

https://www.facebook.com/LMBPNPublishing

https://twitter.com/MichaelAnderle

https://www.instagram.com/lmbpn_publishing/

https://www.bookbub.com/authors/michael-anderle